IT BUBBLES UNDER THE SKIN
Caitlin Marceau

Copyright © 2025 Caitlin Marceau
Cover Art © 2025 Val Halvorson
Interior Art © 2025 Amanda Webb
Edited by Nelka Mazur
First published in 2025 by Hedone Books
ISBN (ebook) 978-1-998664-09-2
ISBN (paperback) 978-1-998664-10-8
ISBN (hardcover) 978-1-998664-11-5

may Violets bloom
wherever you find them

Contents

Content Warning

The story that follows may contain graphic violence and gore.

Please go to the very back of the book for more detailed content warnings.

Beware of spoilers.

One

Jayce inhales sharply as the cold water rushes towards her, the deep blue swallowing everything in its wake as it crashes against the beach. Her skin stings from where the icy tendrils grab at her; although it's almost summer, it's still not warm enough to wade in beyond her ankles.

And yet…

She steadies herself and moves forward, another wave breaking against her exposed skin as she makes her way deeper into the ocean, chasing after the woman who hops happily onward into the bracing waters. She looks up at the sky, her eyes straining as she takes in the sun bright overhead, wishing its rays would warm up more than just the surface. She knows it's just her mind playing tricks on her as she looks down into the blue, but she can't help but think her legs look purple from the cold.

"Are you just going to stand there or are you going to join me, grandma?"

Jayce shakes her head, unable to stop a smile from breaking out across her face. "It's not nice to make fun of the elderly!" she shouts over the noise of the waves.

"You're only two years older than me!" Bridget laughs. Most of her body is now hidden below the surface of the water, her head a golden buoy bobbing in the waves.

"Allegedly! But we both know these bones are old as fuck."

Bridget throws her head back and laughs as a wave hits her. She pulls a face, her nose scrunching up as the corners of her lips pull down in disgust at the salt water that makes its way into her open mouth.

"That's karma for being a bitch!" Jayce shouts at her. She begins to laugh at her partner's misfortune when a large wave that has been gathering momentum finally breaks against her, freezing her to the bone.

"What was that about karma?" her girlfriend calls.

Grumbling, she makes her way over to Bridget, her expression softening as she takes in the other woman's beauty. Her long hair is piled atop her head in a messy bun, though a few of the amber curls have escaped the elastic to gently frame her face. Freckles dance across the bridge of her nose and pepper her cheeks, and Jayce wants nothing more than to kiss each one. As Bridget smiles in the golden light of the afternoon sun, looking like the very goddess she's named after, and when the water crashes against Jayce's body and pushes her back, she realizes that she's breathless not because of the cold, but because of the woman in front of her.

"What are you staring at?" Bridget asks. "Is there something behind me? Am I about to get eaten by a shark?" she jokes, uncomfortable with the attention. She turns away to look at the water in mock horror as Jayce comes up behind her, wrapping her arms tightly around her waist and planting a kiss on the back of her neck.

"As long as I'm the one that gets to eat you, you can call me whatever animal you want."

"I can't believe you said that," Bridget laughs, turning around to stare at her.

Jayce's ears go hot with embarrassment at the lame joke.

"And I can't believe you dragged me into the ocean in the middle of May. Are you trying to kill me?"

"Obviously. How else am I going to cash in on your sweet sweet life insurance policy?"

"Joke's on you, I'm too broke for life insurance."

"Damn. Then what the hell are we doing out here?" Bridget asks, pretending to turn heel and head back towards the shore.

"You tell me!" Jayce laughs, pulling her partner back into her arms as the waves push the two of them closer together.

"I wanted to enjoy the water before it's swarming with tourists," she admits. "This place is going to be crawling with people soon, so I thought it might be nice to enjoy our own private beach while we still can."

Jayce looks over her shoulder and raises an eyebrow at the collection of people on the shore behind them.

"Private?"

"Okay, maybe not *private* private, but definitely more private than it will be in a few weeks."

She makes a good point. Although the Îles de la Madeleine—or "Les Îsles" as the locals call them—was over a day's drive from Montreal, the small cluster of islands would soon be packed to the brim with tourists wanting a taste of small-town life and seaside comforts without the hefty price tag that a vacation to another country—or even another province—could bring. With Canada Day and Saint-Jean-Baptiste right around the corner, a moment like this at Pointe-aux-Loups would soon be rare.

"Yeah, you might have a point," Jayce admits, her eyes fixed on the shore.

"I know I do. Especially since I'm going to be stuck inside the studio for most of the summer too," Bridget says nonchalantly.

It takes a minute for the words to hit Jayce. "The studio?"

"Mhmm."

"Wait, do you mean you g—"

"I got the job!" she shouts, cutting Jayce off in excitement. She breaks free of Jayce's arms and jumps up and down in the waves, tossing her arms over her head and showering them both in saltwater.

"Oh my God!" Jayce shouts, the sand and small pebbles rough underfoot. "I'm so fucking happy for you! I knew you could do it!"

She wraps her arms back around her partner, pulling her close, and planting soft kisses across her skin.

"I'm glad one of us did! I was *positive* I was going to die at the HomeGoods store," she admits.

"Babe, how could they *not* take you? You've been going to that ceramics studio since we were in high school. If they'd given the animator position to anyone else, they would have had a riot on their fucking hands."

"I think you need at least two people to qualify as a riot. But I appreciate the enthusiasm."

"Oh, there would have been. I would have called your mother to come with me."

She makes a horrified face.

"Yeah, you're right. That would have been a riot. I'm glad it didn't come to that."

"I think the whole town is," Jayce says with a laugh. She presses her lips against Bridget's, savouring the taste of the salted caramel kisses of her partner's sweet lip balm mixed with the tang of the salt water. Bridget rests her hands on Jayce's hips, her touch warm in the cold water of the Golfe du Saint-Laurent.

"So when do you start?" Jayce asks, pulling away from Bridget's lips just long enough to come up for air.

Her partner makes a face and looks away with a sigh. "As soon as possible."

"Even with the tourist season still a month away?"

"Yeah. They want to give me enough time to get all the training in, practice leading a few smaller groups ahead of the big rush, and get me to help with inventory before the flood of people."

"Makes sense." Jayce tries to keep the disappointment out of her voice. Although she's excited for her partner, she selfishly wishes she could keep Bridget all to herself throughout the summer.

"Which is why," Bridget muses, dragging out her words, "I thought it might be nice to celebrate today's news with a little fun."

"And you thought giving us both hypothermia was the way to do that?" Jayce asks, dumbfounded.

Bridget flashes Jayce an innocent grin as she slips her fingers underneath Jayce's bikini top. "Don't worry. I'll keep you warm."

She leans in and kisses Jayce, whose lips part ever so slightly for the other woman's tongue, enjoying the way her partner tastes. She moans against her mouth, a shiver running down her spine as Bridget's fingers graze the bottom of Jayce's breast. Her nipples tighten painfully, already hardened by the sea.

"What are you doing?" she asks, shooting the beach a cursory glance. "People might see us."

"People *do* see us, but that doesn't mean they can see what we're doing," she corrects, her thumb and forefinger gently teasing Jayce's nipple. She kisses the crux of Jayce's neck, snaking her other hand down Jayce's back to cup her ass.

"Do you want me to stop?" she asks.

"Fuck no," Jayce says, holding onto her for dear life.

Bridget smiles and continues to let her hands roam, feeling the most intimate parts of Jayce in the cold water. She parts Jayce's legs with her knee, letting go of her ass to trace Jayce's clit through the thin fabric with a finger, the water pressing them against each other and cooling Jayce's suddenly-too-hot body. She inhales sharply as Bridget pulls the fabric of her bikini bottoms to the side and begins rubbing her exposed skin in small circles, working Jayce open before slowly pushing a finger deep inside. Jayce rocks against Bridget, their bodies moving together in rhythm with the current, heat pooling deep within her, her head rolling back in pleasure. Jayce runs a hand up Bridget's back, enjoying the way the other woman's nipples harden against her chest. She undoes the elastic atop Bridget's head, freeing her long locks before burying her fingers in the gold strands. She wants to devour Bridget, drown in her caramel sweetness and sunshine, but she'll settle on just tasting her. She uses her hold on Bridget's hair to guide her lips back to her own.

Briget pumps her fingers into Jayce a little faster and a little rougher. Jayce inhales sharply, caught off guard as a sudden chill grows deep within her. It mixes with the heat of Bridget's fingers, the contrasting sensations making her feel impossibly full as pressure builds deep inside her. She closes her eyes—

—enjoying the warmth of Marguerite's breath against her neck as the two of them pant softly. The fabric of her nightgown is slicked wet and sticks to the other woman's thigh, the white cotton turned translucent. Waves break against the hull, the ship creaking and groaning from the impact.

Her breath hitches in her throat and her heart beats like a war drum, her body moving in rhythm with her lover and the sea as she rubs herself against the thigh that's been positioned between her legs. She runs her fingers through the thick curls gathered at the nape of the other woman's neck, her hair ribbon loosening and falling to the floor.

"I love you," she whispers.—

"I love you," Jayce repeats, the words—the moment—a familiar memory.

Her muscles begin to tense and shake. Something builds deep within, something familiar but more, a sensation that's too much.

"I love you too," Bridget whispers back. "Now come for me."

And Jayce does.

Two

They drive home from the beach in comfortable silence. Jayce gazes out of the window, watching the sand dunes gleam in the afternoon sun. The clouds above are white and fluffy, and the wind carries with it the promise of summer days to come. Yet, despite the warmth inside the small car, Jayce can't shake the cold that's settled deep into her bones. Even though she's bundled in a beach blanket with the heat on high, her body still feels like ice.

Bridget cracks open her window, and Jayce involuntarily lets out a yelp of discomfort. She turns her head towards her partner with a grin, ready to tease her mercilessly at the sound, but when she sees how badly Jayce is shaking and how tightly she's pulled the blanket around her, she changes her mind. She closes the window and accelerates.

And while the drive is short, it feels unnaturally long to Jayce; the normally comfortable vehicle transformed into little more than a rolling freezer.

When the bright blue paint of their small house comes into view, Jayce exhales with relief. The house used to belong to her parents, a vacation home they rented out during the summer months. But as more hotels began cropping up across Les Îles, and tourists began flocking to luxury resorts, Jayce's family found themselves renting the house out less and less as the years went by. Luckily, Jayce was able to convince her parents to sell them the home. The purchase drained most of Jayce's savings, and all of Bridget's, but both of them agreed it was more than worth it.

Thinking of the hot shower waiting for her inside, Jayce throws open the door of the passenger's side before Bridget can even fully park, and rushes up the narrow pathway to the front door. She reaches into her purse, fumbling around for the keyring, before pulling out the silver monstrosity outfitted with more accessories than keys. Her hands shake as she flips through them.

"Do you want me to do that for you?" Bridget calls, catching up to her.

"N-n-no, no. I've g-got it," Jayce replies through chattering teeth, her hands shaking so severely that she misses getting it into the lock on the first few tries, clicking her tongue in frustration when she accidentally leaves a deep scratch on the metal knob. Finally, she manages to fit the key inside the lock. With a soft click, she opens the door and rushes through the entrance straight into the bathroom.

"What if I need to piss?" Bridget laughs, calling after her.

"Then you should have gone in the ocean," Jayce yells back, closing the door behind her.

She crosses the small space and grabs the plastic shower knob, turning it on and twisting it all the way to the left. The shower hisses to life, a curtain of ice water thundering down into the empty tub before the pipes begin to rattle and shake, the cold water quickly turning hot.

The bathroom is small and within minutes, steam fills the space, yet Jayce continues to struggle against the bracing cold that has rooted itself deep within her. She shivers, muscles tensing painfully, as she tries to peel her damp clothes off of her skin. She's never been this cold in her life. It takes a few tries to unbutton her jean shorts, her fingers clumsy from the cold, but once she does she rushes her naked body across the room. She steps into the shower, the porcelain-enameled tub cold against her feet, and pulls the curtain closed. Desperate for warmth, she grabs the showerhead and points it at herself. The realization that she hasn't adjusted the temperature hits her at the same time the scalding water does, and she lets out a scream as the heat lashes at her skin.

Panicked and blinded by pain, she throws her hands up to shield herself and stumbles backward. Her feet slip on the wet surface as she moves too fast with too little traction. She falls, slamming into the towel rack and the edge of the tub, before landing hard on her back, leaving her winded. Water continues to stream down on her, burning her already raw skin. She curls into herself, hands raised in a futile attempt to block the relentless and assaulting heat, yelling in pain and surprise.

The bathroom door bursts open and the shower curtain is yanked open, a panicked Bridget taking in the situation. Quickly, she turns off the water and points the showerhead at the wall before wrapping an arm around Jayce in an attempt to help her up. As she pulls her partner to her feet, Jayce gasps at the sudden contact with her scorched skin.

"Are you okay?" Bridget asks, her voice tight with worry.

"I'll be fine."

"I'm sure you will, but that's not my question. Are you okay *right now?*" she prods again.

Jayce grabs onto both Bridget and the towel rack as she gets to her feet, clinging to them as she waits for her legs to stop shaking before letting go and avoiding the question.

"Jesus, babe," Bridget murmurs, eyes scanning over her naked form. "I think you need to see a doctor."

"It's fine." Jace waves her off. "It's not a big deal."

Bridget frowns. "Babe, you're red. Like, lobster red."

"Well, yeah," Jayce says, forcing a weak smile. "I was at the beach all day and then I got my ass handed to me by a shower. That's not really a surprise."

Bridget doesn't laugh. Instead, she points at Jayce's skin.

Jayce follows her finger, and despite her best efforts, worry creeps in. Angry red splotches mar her skin, a few patches of skin already beginning to swell. She swallows hard.

"Seriously, we should go to the ER."

"No." The response is immediate. "I'm not going to the hospital. Do you know how busy it's going to be?"

Bridget crosses her arms over her chest. "Who cares? You're hurt!"

"I care," Jayce insists. "I don't want to spend twelve hours in an emergency room just to be told to go home, rest, and slap some ointment on it? No thanks."

"Shockingly, I feel like a doctor would give you better advice than that."

Jayce begins to shake, the cold quickly infiltrating the small bathroom once more. "It's not that bad. The skin isn't broken. Nothing's peeling." She forces another smile. "It sucks, and it hurts—so thank you for coming to save my ass—but I'll be fine. Really."

Bridget doesn't look convinced but nods. "Fine. But I'm keeping an eye on you."

Jayce shrugs. "Sure, sounds good."

Bridget hesitates. "You know, even minor burns over a large area can be dangerous."

Jayce doesn't respond. Instead, she turns her attention back to the shower. This time, she keeps the showerhead aimed at the tile as she turns the water on, testing it carefully before stepping under. Relief floods her as the warm water begins chasing away the cold that's coiled inside her, despite the pain each droplet brings. She runs her fingers through her hair, biting her lip against the sudden pain. When she looks at her hands, she notices that both of her palms are covered in red marks. Knowing that Bridget is still hovering nearby she grabs the shampoo and lathers her hair, her face tight with discomfort. She continues washing herself until, eventually, the door closes with a soft click. Jayce exhales with relief and hurries to finish her shower, no longer needing to pretend like she's not in pain. She washes herself quickly and hurriedly gets out of the shower, preparing herself for what she'll see.

She looks down, assessing the damage, and frowns. The burns are worse than she initially thought. In addition to the scalding on her chest and face, the water seems to have hit her left side especially hard. Her shoulder and most of her arm are sore, the skin puffy and uncomfortably tight. Streaks of angry red mark her abdomen and trail over both of her legs. Although no blisters have appeared yet, she swears she can feel them forming, the fluid already gathering between layers of skin.

She glances at the mirror, trying to assess how her face looks, but her reflection is obscured by the steam.

She runs her palm across the glass, her stomach twisting as she catches sight of herself. Her left cheek, the corner of her mouth, and the bridge of her nose are red and puffy. She barely has time to take it in before the steam reclaims the surface.

She wipes the mirror again.

This time, the burns seem worse. The red has spread across more of her face. Her lips look swollen, dotted with angry welts. The skin across her nose appears painfully taut.

Her reflection disappears under the steam once more.

"What the fuck?" she mutters to herself.

She wipes the glass more aggressively, the mirror squeaking beneath her fingers.

This time, her reflection is unrecognizable. Her skin is crimson, grotesquely swollen, her features barely discernible beneath the damage. Her cheeks bulge and her eyes are nearly swollen close, blains creeping over even more of her skin before the reflection disappears from view once more.

Frantically, she scrubs at the mirror, desperate to see herself. But this time, when the glass clears, her face is normal once more. The burns are still there—red streaks across her cheek, jaw, and nose—but they're manageable. *A minor inconvenience*, she tells herself.

Jayce exhales shakily, forcing herself to step away from her reflection as the warmth of the bathroom suddenly becomes suffocating. But the moment she opens the door, she regrets it. Cold air rushes in, seeping into her skin, and sinking deep into her bones. Shivering, she quickly makes her way into the bedroom and gets dressed in warm pajamas, a robe, and a fleece blanket for good measure.

Once she's finished getting changed, she pokes her head into the bathroom just long enough to toss her towels into the hamper. The fog on the mirror has cleared, but she can't bring herself to look at her reflection, afraid it might have changed again.

Instead, she turns away and heads to the living room, curling up on the couch next to Bridget, who waits for her with warm tea and bad reality television.

Three

Jayce scratches her nose, careful not to move too much in case she wakes up Bridget. Her partner lies beside her, snoring softly, her body lying at a diagonal across both of their sides of the bed, her limbs coiled around Jayce. Normally, this would keep her awake, eventually rolling Bridget back onto her side of the bed, rushing to fall asleep before her partner inevitably drifted back over.

But tonight is different.

Tonight, it's not Bridget keeping her up, but rather the cold that's worked its way into her bones. Instead of being an obstacle to her comfort, she's a welcome intrusion. Jayce has always joked that Bridget's blood runs hot and tonight, she's grateful to be right. The warmth from Bridget's body is a lifeline in the frigid, dark room. Jayce pulls the covers taught and focuses on the sound of her partner's breathing, her body instinctively trying to fall in sync with the rhythm of the other woman.

Eventually, she begins to feel sleep pulling at her, and the corners of her mouth lift in a small smile, relieved to finally get some rest after an exhausting day.

Then, from behind her closed eyelids, a light slowly appears. She tries to ignore it, worried that acknowledging it will pull her away from sleep. But it's too late, her attention already shifting to the growing brightness around her. She sighs, wondering how much time she has left before her alarm finally goes off, knowing that if the sun has already risen then she's soon to follow after it.

Resigning herself to waking up, Jayce opens her eyes, only to frown in confusion when she realizes the room in front of her is still pitch dark, the heavy curtains drawn.

That's when it hits her: the light isn't coming from outside. It's coming from behind her, an orange light that flickers and casts shadows on the walls around her. She slowly rolls over in the bed, her breath catching in her throat as she realizes that the light is coming from Bridget.

Jayce sits up in bed, eyes wide, breath catching in her throat. She stares, transfixed on the scene before her, her mouth hanging open in disbelief. Her body trembles, only now it's not from the cold but from the sheer horror of what's unfolding before her.

Bridget's lifeless body burns in the bed beside her.

The flames don't spread to the sheets or lick at Jayce's skin. They cling only to Bridget, devouring her, hollowing her from the inside out. Her pale skin blackens and chars, flaking off and crackling in the heat. The soft, familiar, curves of her body melt away to expose the jagged edges of her partner's bones. Bridget's golden curls are gone, the fire having claimed them before Jayce noticed it had even started. Her full lips and cupid's bow have vanished, replaced by a lipless smile with too many teeth. And then, just as suddenly as the fire started, it stops.

The stench of burnt meat seeps into the air, thick and greasy, creeping into her lungs. Ash coats her tongue and she gags. The realization—the awful, undeniable truth that she now knows what Bridget's flesh tastes like—sends a fresh wave of nausea rolling through her. She clamps a hand over her mouth, unsure if she's trying to keep herself from retching or screaming.

Her breath comes in short, shallow gasps and she reaches out a trembling hand towards her girlfriend, but before she can touch Bridget the corpse suddenly moves. Its head snaps toward her and stares through Jayce with runny eyes.

"You have to let this go," she says in a voice that's not her own.

Jayce panics, desperately scrambling away from Bridget's body. She falls out of bed with a thud, the room exploding with noise: screaming, sobbing, the frantic slapping of her hands and feet against the wooden floor, the loud crash of her wounded body against the heavy nightstand as she thrashes, desperate to get as far away from the corpse as possible.

"Babe, what's wrong?"

Jayce freezes, her heart racing, before mustering enough courage to look over at the bed.

Bridget sits up and watches her with concern.

Jayce can't help the sob that escapes her, relief flooding her body at the sight before her. Bridget is whole again. Her long golden hair tumbles over her shoulders, her skin flushed and healthy, her eyes bright with life. The air in the room is suddenly clear of smoke, the stench of charred flesh gone.

The bedroom is exactly as it should be.

The only thing out of place is Jacye, sprawled on the floor, shaking.

"Babe, what is it?" Bridget throws off the covers and rushes to Jayce's side. She kneels beside her, pulling her into her arms. Jayce clings to her, her raw fingers pressing into Bridget's warm skin, the pain welcome proof that she's real. She presses her face against Bridget's chest, her body wracked with sobs as she cries in relief at the steady, reassuring thump of Bridget's heart.

"Jayce, you're scaring me," Bridget whispers, holding her closer.

"I'm sorry," she chokes out. She tries to steady herself, but the words keep tumbling from her lips, breathless and broken. "I'm sorry. It… It must've been a nightmare, but it felt so real. I don't… I don't know. I—" She stops, swallowing hard and shaking her head. "I'm sorry. I didn't mean to wake you up."

Bridget frowns. "A nightmare? What happened in it?"

Jayce opens her mouth, wanting to be honest but unable to bring herself to say the words.

"I don't know," Jayce lies, gripping her partner a little tighter. "I don't remember."

Bridget doesn't press, she just holds her close and strokes her hair, whispering words of reassurance and love over and over again.

By the time Jayce's breathing evens out, she's already half-asleep in Bridget's arms, her exhaustion winning out over her fear. Although the bed is only a few feet away, it feels impossibly far, and so they stay curled up together on the cold wooden floor, Jayce's body fitting perfectly against Bridget's.

When sleep finally takes her, she prays it's a dreamless one.

Four

Despite getting only a couple of hours of restless sleep, Jayce wakes up before her alarm goes off. She gently untangles herself from Bridget, her body aching. Although she can't see much in the dim morning light that filters into the bedroom, she already knows her burns are worse than she expected and just as bad as Bridget predicted. Her skin is tight and swollen, and she grimaces as she picks herself up, pain shooting through her body.

Jayce pads her way across the bedroom and silently slips into the bathroom. She turns on the light and sits on the toilet, her eyes immediately drawn to the web of blisters across her legs. Under the harsh glow of the fluorescents, she sees them properly for the first time. They're huge, bulbous, and taut with fluid. She lightly touches one with the tip of her finger and a sharp jolt of pain races through her leg.

Although she's still freezing, the thought of wearing pants to work is unbearable. Instead, she mentally makes a note to wear a loose-fitting skirt and a baggy long-sleeve shirt to work today. She flushes and washes her hands, the cool water offering her burnt skin little relief. If anything, it only worsens the ice that's trapped deep inside her from the night before. She dries her hands carefully and takes a long look at herself in the mirror. More blisters have formed overnight, the red splotches from yesterday deepening in color. For a fleeting moment, she worries that her reflection will change like it did the night before—images of swelling skin, spreading welts, and rupturing blisters flash through her mind—but her reflection remains unchanged. She briefly considers calling in sick but dismisses the thought. If she does, Bridget will think she's worse off than she really is. And the last thing she wants is for her partner to worry *again* over her.

With a resigned sigh, she pulls her fleece housecoat tight around her and moves into the kitchen, filling the coffee pot with water before dumping it into the empty tank on the back of the machine. As she scoops coffee into the mesh filter, a pair of arms wrap around her from behind, careful of her sore skin.

"Morning," Bridget murmurs, voice thick with sleep as she presses a kiss to the nape of Jayce's neck.

"Hey. You're up early. Did I wake you?"

"No. I could only sleep on that floor for so long."

Jayce laughs. "Yeah, I know what you mean. I'll never complain about how expensive our mattress was ever a-fucking-gain."

Bridget chuckles and kisses her a second time before stepping back. "How are you feeling?"

Jayce hesitates. If she's honest, Bridget will worry. If she lies, Bridget will see right through her. Instead, she closes the lid of the coffee machine and presses the power button, before turning to face her partner with a halfhearted "Comme ci, comme ça."

Bridget's eyes widen. "Jesus Christ, you're a fucking mess."

Jayce frowns. She should have known Bridget would worry no matter what.

"Babe, you have to call in sick today."

"I can't."

"You have to. You can't go to work like this."

"I have to."

"What the hell are you talking about? It's not your coffee house! Of course you can! And you should!" she argues.

"I'm on the morning shift and the earliest anyone can come in is around lunch. Denise is on vacation before the summer rush. Aaron's busy with finals. You know how it is this time of the year. Besides, it's not even seven. I doubt anyone's even awake enough to take a call, let alone replace me," she reasons with a shrug.

Bridget crosses her arms. "It's just a job, Jayce. Your health should come first."

"I know it's just a job, but I care about it. I enjoy it. And I'm fine!"

Bridget sighs, exasperated. "Babe, if you sat out in the yard, people would think I left out a Halloween decoration from last fall."

Jayce snorts. "Wow. I feel so pretty. Thanks."

"I'm serious. You look like shit!"

"I know," Jayce says curtly. "And I'll look like shit for a while. But I still have to go to work."

Bridget throws her hands up in frustration, knowing an unwinnable fight when she sees one. "Whatever. At the very least, let me put some ointment on you before you get dressed."

Jayce nods, the coffee percolating behind her, and she heads back into the bathroom with Bridget fast on her heels. She swings open the medicine cabinet and grabs a small bottle of painkillers, popping the lid off with a loud click. She tosses two aspirin into her mouth, swallowing them dry. The pills stick to her throat on the way down, acidic and bitter, and she shudders as her throat suddenly feels raw. She moves to snap the lid back onto the bottle, but in her haste, she catches a raw patch of skin between the plastic rim and the cap.

"Son of a bitch," she hisses, dropping the bottle. It clatters into the sink, pills spilling across the bottom of the white porcelain basin. She shakes her stinging hand in the air, muttering obscenities under her breath.

A hand reaches out, gently taking her blistered palm. For a split second, she thinks it's Bridget but realizes that the fingers are too long, too thin, too delicate. A rush of fear surges through her, but she can't bring herself to pull away. Instead, she looks up slowly and scans the face of the unfamiliar woman. Her eyes trace the sharp curve of her nose, the striking angle of her cheekbones, and the fullness of her rose lips. The woman smiles—her grin full of good humour—and lifts Jayce's hand to her lips, turning it over and pressing a kiss to her fingertip.

"Better?" she asks.

Jayce opens her mouth, heart pounding, a million questions galloping through her mind. But instead of asking anyone of them, the only thing that comes out is a breathless—

—*"Yes. Thank you."*

"Good," Marguerite says before letting go of Claudine's hand. "You need to be more careful."

"I know," Claudine admits, folding her hands in her lap, savouring the way Marguerite's lips felt against her skin. She looks down, a small red dot blooming where the pin pricked her skin. "How is it that I've been sewing for years and I'm still so bad at it?"

Marguerite laughs, her hands quickly working the needle and thread even when her eyes are fixed elsewhere. "You're not especially bad at it.*"*

"I'm just not very good either.*"*

"You could stand to get better," Marguerite teases.

"God help me, do I know it."

"At least you're good with your garden."

"I'm amazing with my garden," Claudine jokes.

The two women chuckle before continuing their work in comfortable silence. The room is small and plain, its wooden floors and walls sparsely decorated. Claudine tries to relax in the chair, but today it feels too stiff. She sits ramrod straight, unable to settle into the seat. Though it's spring and the windows are open, the room feels stifling and her skin is too warm. Marguerite has always had this effect on her, even when they were younger. But ever since the two of them had grown into young women, Claudine has found herself even more nervous around Marguerite's familiar face.

A bead of sweat rolls down her back and she shivers.

In front of them, a small heap of clothing sits on the floor: socks, linen slips, aprons, and other small pieces needing minor repairs. Although everyone knows Claudine is clumsy with a needle, stabbing herself as often as she stabs the fabric, they insist she practice. Marguerite, on the other hand, has always been naturally adept with a needle and thread and so she helps earn her keep, bringing in petty cash with her skills to help her parents' ever-growing family.

The second oldest of five girls, she carries the weight of responsibility with quiet grace.

But Claudine imagines she won't have to worry about being another mouth to feed for much longer; not with her betrothed returning home from war. Soon, Marguerite will begin a new life in a new town with a stranger she barely knows. And while Claudine is happy for her friend's future, she dreads the fact that she'll soon be mourning what they once had. In some ways, she knows she's already begun.

"When does François get back?" Claudine asks.

Discussing Marguerite's soon-to-be husband is normally a topic she avoids, but she wants to be ready for his arrival so her curiosity wins out over self-preservation.

"Any day now," Marguerite says, her voice flat despite the smile she wears. "I hear the battle has been won, and the men are coming home. So I imagine once he arrives, our wedding will shortly follow."

"Oh. That's… that's good."

"Yes, I suppose it is."

Claudine thinks she hears a note of sadness in Marguerite's voice, but she doesn't dare comment. Instead, she wipes her forehead with the back of a hand, her cheeks flushed, and turns her attention back to her work.

"I need to be off," Marguerite eventually says, finishing off her last stitch. "Mother will be home from the market soon, and I'm sure she'll need help preparing supper."

"Oh, of course. I should probably start on dinner, too," she lies, knowing that there's not much to prepare. Tonight's meal will be the same as yesterday's: bread and salted meat.

Marguerite removes the linen square from its small wooden frame, and Claudine finally catches a glimpse of her work. It's a handkerchief, adorned with her initials and surrounded by a decorative braid.

"That's beautiful," Claudine says.

"Thank you. It's a gift for François."

Her heart sinks.

"My mother said it's customary to give a man a handkerchief before he leaves for war," Marguerite explains. "Unfortunately, I had nothing to give François when he left and so she suggested I make him something for his return."

"How thoughtful of you."

"Yes, how very thoughtful of her," Marguerite corrects.

She gathers her things into a small straw basket at her feet. As she stands, so too does Claudine.

"Before you leave, I need to give you something," Claudine blurts, her heart pounding.

"Oh?"

"One moment," she says, rushing into the other room. "Don't go anywhere!" she calls. After a few moments, she returns with a small linen square of her own, the cloth folded in her hands. It's a handkerchief, but unlike Marguerite's, the stitching is clumsy, the work of hands that lack any real talent. A small bouquet of purple violas and ochre leaves decorate the corners of the fabric. She carries it delicately between both hands like an anxious child before extending it to the other woman.

"You made this for me?" Marguerite asks, her voice soft. "This must have cost you a fortune to get," she says, running a thumb over the purple thread.

Blood rushes to Claudine's ears. If she thought she was warm before, it's nothing compared to the heat that floods her face now.

"Well, it's not very good," she laughs nervously. "I needed to practice, and I can only make so many of these for myself." Marguerite stares at her, lost in thought, and Claudine's mouth is suddenly too dry. "I just… I wanted you to have it. Since you and François will be leaving soon…" She looks at the ground unable to finish the sentence. "Well, at any rate, they say marriage is a type of war, don't they? So I wanted you to have this so you can remember me in the heat of battle."

"Thank you." Her voice is thick with sincerity, and the kindness in it catches Claudine off guard. She smiles, still unable to meet Marguerite's eyes, focusing instead on the floor. A strand of her hair falls loose, slipping in front of her face. As though compelled by instinct, Marguerite reaches out, her delicate fingers tucking it behind Claudine's ear.

It's enough to make Claudine feel brave, and so she looks up to meet the other woman's gaze—

—only to find herself staring at the once-more burnt corpse of Bridget. It looks back at her with a pained expression, mouth open in a perpetual scream, its eyelids missing. The corpse holds Jayce's injured finger to its lipless mouth, pressing white teeth against her skin in a silent kiss, its hand charred and withered, the fingers stiff as smoke rises from the burnt limb.

Reflexively, Jayce pulls her hand away, clutching it to her chest as she jumps back. A jolt of pain radiates through her hip as she slams against the sink, the impact sending a sharp ache up her back and down her legs. For a moment, she thinks her knees might buckle.

"Are you okay?" Bridget asks, her brows knit with concern as she studies Jayce. Much like the night before, her body is restored in an instant, her burnt husk nowhere to be seen.

"Yeah, I'm fine," she says quickly, breathing hard and fast as if she's just run a marathon. "Sorry, I guess my skin's more sensitive than I thought."

Bridget glances down at Jayce's hands and inhales sharply, grimacing at the fresh blisters forming along her partner's skin. "Oh, I'm sorry. I wasn't thinking—"

"No, no, you're fine," Jayce interrupts, staring hard at the floor. She's afraid that if she looks at Bridget again, she'll see a charred corpse instead of the woman she loves.

Bridget reaches out again, gently cupping Jacye's chin and tilting her face upward before pressing a soft kiss to her lips. A wave of relief washes over Jayce when she sees that Bridget is still whole, her skin unmarred.

"Here, at the very least, let me get your back while I'm still here," she says, breaking their kiss and reaching into the open medicine cabinet to grab a tube of ointment.

"Thanks."

Jayce turns around and lifts her shirt, the cool salve making her shiver as Bridget spreads it carefully across her skin. Thankfully, there aren't too many blisters on her back, and Bridget makes quick work of them. "Want me to do the rest?" she asks, eyes roaming over the rest of her partner's body.

"No, I'll get them. Thanks though."

She passes Jayce the open tube, planting another kiss on her lips and flashing a worried smile before stepping out, leaving her alone in the enclosed space once more. She exhales shakily as she applies the medication to the rest of her burns. The sting is sharp at first, but as the salve settles, it soothes the raw skin.

When she reaches her hip, she frowns. Pain pulses through the area, and as she lowers the waistband of her boxer shorts, she grimaces. The blisters that should have been there are ruptured, leaving behind pale, flattened skin and trails of moisture glistening down her leg. She clicks her tongue against her teeth, annoyed. The impact against the sink must have burst them. As she brushes her fingers over the empty pockets of skin, she realizes they're not just wet, but still slowly leaking fluid. With a sigh, she grabs a small box of bandages from the medicine cabinet, meticulously peeling open the paper wrappers and adhesive tabs. She lines up the brown fabric strips, carefully covering the exposed skin. By the time she's done, exhaustion weighs heavily on her. More than anything, she wants to crawl back into bed and sleep. But she knows that if she takes any longer, she'll be late for work. With a resigned sigh, she puts everything back in its place, shuts the medicine cabinet, and leaves the bathroom to get ready for the day.

Five

The drive to work is a quiet one. This early in the morning and during the off-season, Jayce hardly encounters other cars on the road. She passes the campus for the Cégep de la Gaspésie et des Îles and smiles, remembering her time in school.

Although the coffee shop isn't technically on the campus itself, it's close enough that it's frequented almost entirely by students. At this time of the year, they're more often than not in a panic about upcoming exams, looming deadlines, and encroaching course selections. She expects today will be no different, with the bulk of her customers being students in distress as their semester comes to a close. But soon, the frantic students will be replaced by equally frantic professors, trying to get their grading in before the deadline.

She parks her car and makes her way across a small parking lot to the coffeehouse door, keys in hand. Although she'd never been a fan of academia, she'd be lying if she said she didn't enjoy the environment it brings; the tall buildings, the studious atmosphere, the library full of books, and the access to endless resources for information. While she has no intention of going back to school—truthfully, the idea of running her own coffeehouse appeals to her more than higher education—she can't help but miss the ambiance that comes with bustling student life.

Jayce fiddles with the key ring, looking through the jumbled collection with aching fingertips. Just as she goes to unlock the coffeehouse, she hears a sound that paralyzes her: the crashing of waves.

Normally, the sound of the ocean would be a welcome and relaxing one. But this far inland causes alarm bells to ring in her head. She looks around, confused, but sees only the cold asphalt of the empty parking lot. She shakes her head, trying to clear her thoughts, pushing aside the sudden surge of panic. Her hand is shaking and poised at the keyhole when there's another thunderous roar as waves crash against something solid. Jayce's eyes widen in shock as water begins to creep in around her, cold droplets splashing against her legs and pooling around her bare feet.

Wait, where the fuck did my shoes go?

She looks down, confused, and she hisses in a sudden jolt of pain—

—as her leg hits the side of the stair. Claudine struggles for purchase, trying to get her feet underneath her as she's dragged up the wet wooden steps.

The ship creaks, water slamming against the hull, sea foam spraying high into the air and soaking through the thin linen of her nightgown. Below deck, she can hear Marguerite yelling and struggling against another person as they attempt to drag her upstairs too. Claudine stumbles, falling forward, but strong arms lift her before she can hit the ground, dragging her up onto the deck of the ship.

A group of men stand clustered together, and although their expressions range from quiet rage to blistering hate, they all have one thing in common: eyes gleaming with violent intent. Had Claudine not spent the last few weeks aboard the ship with them, she wouldn't have been able to recognize them as members of the crew. She opens her mouth to plead for help, but the wind is knocked out of her before she gets a chance as she's thrown hard to the ground, seawater splashing around her. She shivers and gasps for air, her body shaking.

One of the men leans over and grabs her hands roughly.

"Stop! Get off of me!" Claudine tries to pull away, but his grip only tightens, her bones threatening to snap beneath his tremendous strength. She continues

to shout as a rough length cord is wrapped excruciatingly taut around her wrists before another man grabs her legs and binds her ankles.

She writhes on the ground, struggling against her bonds as the men yell and spit at her. Somewhere behind her, she can hear Marguerite pleading with someone to let Claudine go.

"We shouldn't have taken them aboard," one of them says.

"I told you it was bad luck to sail with women," says another.

"They're cursed!" someone shouts.

"We're being tested!" another chimes in.

An oil lamp clutched in one man's hands flickers, painting the faces of the mob in deep, ever-shifting reds. "We are being judged for their sins," he says. "If we want to make it to port, we need to atone. And they need to be punished."

Marguerite is thrown onto the deck beside her. Before the men can tie her feet, she kicks out, struggling wildly against them, and they give her space like they would any other cornered animal. A few of them laugh and pretend to lunge at her, clearly enjoying the panic in her eyes. Claudine watches as the ring of men around Marguerite gets a little smaller, their eyes alight with rage. Her heart, already pounding, threatens to burst.

"No!" Claudine shouts. "She didn't do anything! It was me! Me alone! I seduced her! Please! I'm the only one that deserves to be punished! Please!"

"You're right," a man beside her hisses. She recognizes him; his face had been kind and gentle when he had helped her aboard the ship. It was nothing like that now. "You do deserve to be punished." He grabs the front of her nightgown, hoisting her up.

"Please!" Marguerite cries. "Have mercy!"

Claudine struggles against the man as he drags her toward the edge of the ship.

"No! Please don't!" she screams, her voice catching in her throat as he lifts her off the ground, her legs banging against the ship's railing. The ocean churns below her, the water black and unforgiving, and Claudine is filled so full of terror that she can't find it in her to feel shame as a trail of wet warmth runs down her thigh. "No! Please! No!" she cries.

"Claudine!" Marguerite yells, her voice a wail of despair as the men close in, ropes in hand.

Claudine breathes fast, bile rising in the back of her throat she looks down.

Behind her, someone screams—

"Hey, are you guys going to be opening soon?"

Jayce snaps back to reality. She clutches her chest, her heart racing, her breath too fast. She looks around, panicked, trying to find Marguerite before remembering where she is. The sound of the waves is gone and in their place is the silence only early morning can bring.

"What?" she asks the stranger, struggling to focus.

"Are you guys opening soon? If not, I can always come back later."

"Oh. Yeah. Sorry."

Remembering herself, she unlocks the door and makes her way behind the counter, turning on machines and setting up for the day.

She glances at the clock on the register and stops.

8:47 a.m.

That can't be right.

She rummages through her purse and pulls out her phone.

8:47 a.m.

Was I really just standing here for almost an hour?

"Hey, can I order now?" the customer asks awkwardly from the counter.

"Oh, yeah! I'm so sorry. I'll be with you in just a moment," Jayce says, tying on her apron and getting to work.

Six

As Jayce works, the pain from her blisters becomes a constant dull throb that makes even the smallest task unpleasant, but it quickly becomes apparent that her physical discomfort isn't the worst obstacle her shift brings.

It's the customers and their constant stares as they pretend not to look at the swollen welts spread across her face.

Although she tries to ignore them at first, her blisters are more than just the subject of awkward small talk but a deterrent for would-be customers. People stare too long, hesitate at the counter, and some turn away altogether when they see her. At first, she thinks they're overreacting, but when she catches her reflection in the polished metal of the milk frother, it takes everything in her not to recoil. The blisters are bigger and cover even more of her skin. They bulge, pulsating as though alive, the grotesque pustules threatening to erupt at any moment.

When two girls enter, catch sight of her, and immediately exit, she knows something has to be done. As frustrating as it is, she can't blame them. Who wants their coffee made by someone who looks like a walking communal disease?

Swallowing her pride, Jayce retreats to the backroom and

rummages through a supply box until she finds a box of disposable face masks. The rough fabric scrapes against the blisters as she secures it over her nose and mouth, making her wince. A sharp, stinging pain flares across her face and she sucks in a steadying breath, squaring her shoulders in resignation and making her way back out to the register.

The mask helps. Sort of. Although it conceals the majority of the damage, it doesn't stop the unending small talk.

"Oh no, are you sick?"

"Are you contagious?"

"I hope you feel better soon!"

The shift crawls forward, which does little to relieve Jayce's sluggishness and disorientation. Normally, work keeps her too busy to feel tired or to lose herself in thought. Today, though, it feels like an unending expanse of time, a liminal space holding Jayce hostage as she prays for the end of her shift. It makes her uneasy.

With her clientele thinned—the usual rush of students having never arrived—the shop feels eerily empty and static. The quiet should be a relief, but it isn't.

As Jayce thinks of productive ways to spend the remainder of her day, she realizes that something isn't right. A pain she'd been attributing to her blisters begins to grow and swell. It's deep in her abdomen—a low, rolling pressure that grows stronger in small surges—and feels like her body is tying itself in knots.

Then the first spasm hits.

Sharp, searing, sudden. It's a pain so intense it steals her breath and buckles her knees, her white-knuckle grip on the counter the only thing keeping her from tumbling to the floor. And just like that, it stops.

Period cramps?

She shakes her head, dismissing it.

Waaaaay too early.

Fifteen minutes later, blinding pain rips through her again.

She gasps, dropping a handful of coins as a customer looks on nervously, the silver disks scattering across the floor. The pain lances through her, sharper this time as she bends in half, scrambling for the fallen change, each movement sending fresh jolts of agony through her core. As she picks up the last of the fallen coins, the cramps suddenly stop…

Only to come back a few minutes later while frothing milk.

And again when plating a croissant.

And again while taking a new order.

And again and again and again.

This feels like labour.

The thought is absurd and impossible, and Jayce would laugh it off if it wasn't for the way the pain comes in waves, as predictable as the tide, swelling and crashing over her in intervals that feel impossibly timed.

The next cramp—*contraction, no, no, not a contraction*—hits her hard. She grips the register with both hands, worried that she's going to rip it off of the counter, her breath ragged and fast as she rides it out. She squeezes her eyes shut, tears welling behind her lashes, willing it to stop. And as suddenly as the pain started, it vanishes. She holds her breath, anticipating another wave of agony, but it never comes.

Jayce prays it stays that way.

Seven

Much to Jayce's relief, the cramps stay away for the remainder of the next hour, her shift passing in a predictably calm rhythm. Although the pain from her blisters continues to swell, she welcomes the discomfort over the mind-numbing pain from before.

When the last customer finally leaves Jayce retreats into the back room and steals a moment for herself. She squats low to the floor, wrapping her arms around her legs as she rests her forehead against her knees, breathing deep and slow. Her hip feels itchy, and she absentmindedly scratches at it, only remembering the blisters when she rakes her nails across them. She hisses, pulling a face from the jolt of pain and the unexpected fluid that coats her fingers.

"What the fuck?" she mutters, standing up and twisting awkwardly, trying to look at her backside to see where the moisture is coming from.

She runs her fingertips over her skirt and when they come back wet, she realizes with a start that the bandages she put on this morning must have fallen off. She tugs her skirt down to expose her hip and feels around for the loose bandages, instead finding them exactly where she'd stuck them on, only now completely soaked through.

"Disgusting," she mutters, using the tip of her nail to lift one of the corners enough for her to grab it with her fingers, sucking in a sharp breath as she tears the small rectangular patch off her skin before repeating the process with the rest of them.

She twists her neck around again, trying once more to get a look at her backside, when she sees something that makes her stomach curdle.

The fabric of her skirt is stained, a trail of wetness leads from the back of her hip bone to nearly halfway down the back of her thigh. Rings of white radiate from the damp patch of cotton. She runs her fingers along the outline and recognition dawns on her as she feels the soft grit; they're the same ones she gets on her boots during wintertime.

Salt.

What the fuck?

The ruptured blisters themselves are as she remembers them from this morning: flat white pockets of dead skin, damp from the drained fluid. While they should have dried out by now, Jayce realizes that water is still dribbling out of them.

That's fucking impossible.

She places a hand over the remnants of the blisters and presses lightly, horrified when one of them begins to seep.

How?

She crosses the small room to a roll of brown paper towels and grabs several sheets, pressing them firmly to her hip as she scans the room, quickly locating the red first aid kit mounted on the back wall. She takes out a bandage and presses it onto her skin. As she takes out a second one, the first begins to slip down her skin, its adhesive coming loose. She grabs it before it slides further down her hip, horrified to see that the tan fabric is already soaked through, the fluid seeping out of the blisters faster now. She tries again with a second bandage and is unsurprised when she's met with the same outcome.

She reaches back into the first aid kit, this time pulling out a sterile square of gauze. She rips open the paper package and pulls out the thick square, surprised by the unfamiliar texture she was expecting. This is folded in on itself, and as she opens it up her heart beats fast in disbelief as she realizes that it's a handkerchief, not gauze, that's been hiding in the package.

She turns the linen over in her hands, rubbing a thumb across one of the embroidered bouquets of violas. As she looks at it, small drops of water begin appearing on the fabric. She looks up, frowning—

—at the tears that fall onto the handkerchief clutched between her and Marguerite.

She lets out a shaky breath, and Claudine gently pulls the linen out of Marguerite's hand, folding it up, and using it to blot away the tears that bead down the woman's cheeks. Claudine wants to comfort her friend, but she can't. She doesn't know what to say in a situation like this, so she lets silence fill the space meant for reassuring words.

Marguerite lets out another shaky exhale. "François' really dead," she says. "A letter was brought home to his family last night, and they gave it to me this morning confirming his passing on the battlefields."

"I'm sorry," Claudine says. She opens her mouth to say more, then quickly closes it. All she can think to say is sorry and, if she's being honest, she isn't. The thought fills her with shame and revulsion. She knows Marguerite is mourning her would-be husband, but Claudine can't help but selfishly be happy that Marguerite gets to stay with her a little while longer. "I wish I knew what to tell you," Claudine finally admits. "I wish I knew how to comfort you right now. I'm sorry for your loss. I know it's horrible, but you're stronger than this moment. You're kind, and beautiful, and warm, and I know you'll find someone to love in no time at all. I know you will and—

A sound bursts from Marguerite's lips, something trapped between a sob and a chuckle. She presses the white handkerchief against her lips as if embarrassed to be saying the words coming out of her mouth.

"I'm not," Marguerite says quietly.

"What?"

"I'm not sorry," Marguerite repeats, her voice hardly above a whisper. "Isn't that horrible? Aren't I despicable? The man who would have been my husband was killed, and I'm not sad about it." Her voice is monotone, her eyes distant, fixed on something far away. "I know I should be. Any good woman would be devastated. And I know my family needed this, but I'm..." she hesi-

tates, wringing the handkerchief nervously. "I'm happy. I didn't want to marry him."

The silence between them swells and Marguerite shifts her weight nervously from one foot to the other, unable to meet the other woman's eyes.

Eventually, Claudine speaks.

"I didn't want you to marry him either."

She tries to sound detached, but there's unmistakable desperation in her voice as the words leave her mouth. Despite being draped in a long dress and apron, she feels naked and exposed, her soul bare for Marguerite. The thought of being seen so completely terrifies her. Claudine looks away, her cheeks flushed with embarrassment, but Marguerite reaches out and cups her face, turning it towards her as she steps closer, the soft handkerchief pressed between her warm hand and Claudine's warmer skin.

Marguerite is silent as she looks at Claudine, her eyes tracing the lines of her face, taking in the fullness of her lips, the sharpness of her brow, the dark locks of hair threatening to spill from beneath her bonnet. Wherever her gaze lands, Claudine's skin burns. She wants to pull away, the sensation almost too much to bear. But the thought of breaking this connection, of severing whatever fragile bond has formed between them, is unthinkable. Marguerite's thumb gently traces Claudine's lower lip, and her mouth parts at the touch, a small sigh escaping. Claudine places her hands over Marguerite's, though she's not sure if it's to steady herself or anchor the other woman to her. Before she has time to figure it out, Marguerite leans in and presses her lips against her.

Claudine savors the taste of Marguerite: sweet honey and tart apples.

Footsteps approach the house from outside, and the two women steal another kiss before quickly pulling apart just as the door bursts open—

—"What the hell are you doing?"

Jayce spins around, startled, knocking over the first aid kit as the backroom door swings open. Bandages, gloves, and medical supplies scatter around her feet, and she grumbles to herself in annoyance.

"Are you hurt?" River asks as they look at the red bag on the counter, before turning their attention to Jayce, their eyes widening when they see the blisters covering her skin. "Jesus Christ, what the fuck happened to you?"

"It's a long story."

"Do you need me to call you an ambulance or something?"

"No no, it's fine. It didn't happen here," Jayce reassures them. "I burnt myself in the shower at home and my bandage came off. The place was empty, so I thought I'd take a second to put on a new one."

"Empty?" River asks in disbelief.

"Yeah."

"I don't know how long you've been back here, but the place is fucking *packed* and there's a long line at the cash." Jayce looks at the clock on the wall, her stomach sinking when she spots the time. She's been in the backroom for over an hour.

"Sorry, I didn't realize. I guess an exam must have just ended," she lies.

"Don't worry about it. I'll jump on the register until you're good," River says with a concerned smile as they head back out into the shop.

"Sounds good," she calls after them.

Jayce looks down at her hand. The handkerchief is gone and in its place, she holds a gauze square. She presses it against her hip, wincing at the pain, before picking up the roll of medical tape off of the floor. She tears off a few strips of the adhesive with her teeth, before securing the gauze against herself as best she can. She repeats the process a few more times, making sure to cover as many of the weeping sores as she can. It's a clumsy job, but it'll have to do.

She scans the room one more time, making sure everything is cleaned up, before heading out to help River, the taste of honey and apples still on her lips.

Eight

"Are you okay in there?" River asks, their voice muffled by the thick wood of the bathroom door.

"Yeah, I'll be fine," Jayce says, her voice breaking, robbing the statement of what little credibility it had. She sits on the toilet, the plastic seat cold against her skin, and presses her forehead against her knees, breathing heavily into the fabric of her skirt that she's gathered around her legs. Her abdomen clenches, waves of pain shooting up her back and down her legs, the agonizing cramps from before suddenly back with renewed intensity. She balls her hands into fists despite the painful blisters covering her skin. Her muscles relax just long enough for her to feel safe before tightening up again, the stabbing cramps unbearable.

"Fuck," she hisses to herself, trying to catch her breath. She pulls at the roll of toilet paper, ripping off a few squares and balling them up in her hand before reaching it between her legs and dabbing at herself. When she looks down at the used paper, it comes away wet, but absent of blood.

Knowing she can't hide in the small bathroom forever, she finishes up and tries to make herself presentable, avoiding the mirror at all costs. It takes a surprising amount of effort to move, her body wracked with pain, and by the time she reaches the door, she's already out of breath.

"You really look like shit," River tells her as she steps out.

"Yeah, I know," she groans.

She makes her way past clusters of tables and cozy chairs and is almost at the register when another wave crashes over her, driving her to her knees. Her arms wrap tightly around her stomach, muscles tensing as bile rises in the back of her throat. She closes her eyes, breathing in through her nose and out through her mouth, trying to clear her head. For a moment, she thinks she's going to throw up, but after a moment the nausea and cramping stop.

Jayce doesn't realize River has moved to her side until their hands are already on her back, rubbing small circles against her skin. It's a kind gesture, and Jayce knows they mean well, but she can't stop the cry of pain that escapes her as their hand brushes against tender blisters they didn't know were there, a dull ache radiating from the spot.

River quickly removes their hand, pulling a face. Jayce watches, confused by their reaction, when she begins to feel a trickle roll down her back. She reaches a hand behind herself and touches her shirt, her fingers coming away damp from bursting blisters.

"I'm so sorry!" River says, their hands hovering awkwardly over her skin.

"Don't worry about it."

"I really didn't mean to hurt you!"

"It's fine," she says through gritted teeth. "You were just trying to help."

Once she catches her breath, Jayce uses the counter to pull herself up to her feet, before stumbling into the backroom to hang up her apron and grab her purse.

"I think I need to go home," Jayce says apologetically. "I really don't feel well. Is that okay? Like, will you be fine here until the evening shift gets in?"

"Yeah, don't worry about it. Just take care of yourself."

"Thanks."

As Jayce makes her way back around the counter, she reaches up and clumsily grabs at her face mask, hooking her finger through one of the elastic ear loops and pulling it off in one quick motion. The rough fabric drags against the tender wounds on her face. There's an eruption of small pops, firecrackers being set off under her skin, as a trail of blisters across the bridge of her nose ruptures.

"Fuck!" she yells, resisting the urge to cup her face with her hands as she stumbles toward a small island near the door, grabbing at a stack of napkins with trembling hands. She presses the napkins against her skin, patting gently to absorb the leaking fluid that trails down her face. It beads down her neck and drips onto her shirt. A trickle of water dribbles off the tip of her nose and onto her lips. She wipes it away, but an all-too-familiar smell fills the air and lingers around her: that of the ocean.

Pain from her abdomen slams into her again, spurring her to action. She stumbles out of the door and across the parking lot to her car. With a pained grunt, she gets inside and starts the engine, bracing herself for the short but unbearable drive home.

Nine

The campus shrinks in the rearview mirror, while her view of the ocean ahead grows more striking with each passing minute. Although she's eager to get home, she's grateful for the respite that comes when she reaches a red light. Jayce rests her temple against the steering wheel, exhaling slowly as she tries to calm her breathing, before looking up to admire the sweeping view of the Golfe de Saint-Laurent. It's breathtakingly blue, the water sparkling in the bright sun, and it stretches endlessly before her. The water remains as restless as ever, waves of deep sapphire picking up speed, swelling high before crashing against the pale beaches.

The spring air is crisp and biting, and she fights the urge to roll down her window. Normally, she welcomes the sting of cold air against her cheeks, but today, with her raw face, it would be excruciating. Even with the windows closed, the taste of salt is heavy in the air. She closes her eyes, inhaling deeply—

—enjoying the smell. Although she's spent most of her life only a few hours away from the water, it's her first time seeing the sea.

The ship docked ahead of her is enormous, and Claudine swears its mast is big enough to pierce the heavens. The massive wooden structure looms over the port, dwarfing the people that swarm the docks like rats, scurrying around each other as they make their way on and off the great vessel. Along the stern is the ship's name: Le Saint-Clément. The letters are massive and painted red, weathered by salt water and sun. The waves slap against the hull of the ship, a sound she never realized could be so deafening, especially when mixed with the chatter of voices, the creaking of timber, and the muffled thuds of cargo being hauled across the docks. Her pulse thumps in her ears, her heart quickening. Looking up at its towering spars and endless rigging, she suddenly feels small again, and like a child, she wishes she could hide behind her mother's skirts. The journey ahead of her feels too big, too vast, too much. Bile rises in the back of her throat as her nerves get the better of her. She grips the side of the wagon, her knuckles going white, trying to still them from shaking.

Her father's horse trudges forward, pulling the small cart that carries Claudine, her trunk of belongings, and a few goods for the market. She wishes the rest of her family were here to see her off, desperate for one last embrace or reassuring touch. But with warm weather finally upon them, the farm can't spare extra hands; not when there's so much planting to be done. Her father brings the horse to a stop and dismounts, taking a moment to admire the view before turning to her. He lifts her trunk from the wagon and, with a quiet nod, escorts both her and her belongings toward the dock's edge.

As they approach, a crewman spots them and hurries over, taking the trunk from her father's hands.

"We'll be departing sooner than expected," the man says, his voice thin and reedy, but his face kind. The corners of his eyes wrinkle as he smiles, an obvious attempt to calm the visibly nervous Claudine. "We want to take advantage of the winds while we still can. One of the crew will give you a tour of the ship once we embark, but for now, just know that you'll be staying below deck with the other Filles du Roi. Each of you has a small cabin and I'll see to it that your trunk is placed in your quarters."

"Much thanks," Claudine's father answers for her, extending his hand. The crewman takes it and gives it a single firm shake. His skin is tanned from hours spent under the sun, his palms cracked from labor at sea. Without another word, he hoists Claudine's belongings onto his shoulder and makes his way onto the ship.

"I suppose this is where we part ways," her father says, a sad smile on his face.

"Yes."

His brow furrows. "And you're sure you want this? To start your life in Nouvelle-France?"

It's not an unexpected question. She knew he'd ask her one final time before she set sail. What does surprise her is her sudden reluctance to answer it. Her voice catches somewhere deep in her throat, the words lost in the back of her mouth.

The voyage ahead will be brutal, as all sea journeys are. And while many women before her have made this passage to the colonies, many have also died en route, their bodies swallowed up by the sea before ever reaching them. She wants to be brave, but it's impossible to know what's really waiting for her in those foreign lands, though—like everyone—she's heard the stories of wild terrain and wilder beasts.

But if she stays in France…

Her skin feels suddenly too tight, her breath trapped in her lungs. She scans the crowd ahead of her, trying to ground herself.

If she stays, she knows what kind of life she'll have. Her family will find her a suitable husband, one who would be kind and would provide for her. She'd have children, a home, and a future in a small town nestled in a quiet province, in a country she's always known.

It would be a good life.

A predictable life.

She's tempted—so tempted—to tell her father that she wants to go home. That she's making a mistake and wants the safety that comes with certainty.

And then her eyes find Marguerite. She leans against the side of the ship, looking out at her brother-in-law and older sister, who watch her from the pier.

Warmth washes over her, steadying her. It excites her just as much as it anchors her. And suddenly, despite the uncertainty—or maybe because of it—she knows she wants to go. As long as Marguerite is with her, she knows she'll be okay.

"Yes," she finally tells him. "I'm sure."

Her father exhales, nodding once. "Be safe," he says, wrapping her in a strong embrace before pressing a kiss to her forehead. "Send letters when you can."

"I will. I love you, Father."

He opens his mouth as if to give some final fatherly advice, but stops *himself. "You should be off," he says instead, his voice tinged with sadness. "Safe travels."*

She offers him one last smile before turning away, stepping carefully across the wooden planks, and making her way onto the boat. She takes a spot on the deck beside Marguerite, the other woman's face lighting up at Claudine's arrival, and it's not long before the crew lifts anchor and the ship begins to drift from the docks, its massive sails catching the wind.

Claudine and Marguerite—as well as the other Filles du Roi who've taken spots on the deck alongside them—lean over the railing, waving goodbye to family, friends, and other onlookers who watch the ship begin its long journey.

Out of the corner of her eye, Claudine catches a streak of white and she realizes that Marguerite is waving the linen handkerchief that Claudine gave her. She can't help but smile at the sight and take in the other woman's beauty: the softness of her lips, the excitement in her eyes, the long locks of black that swirl around her in the winds of the Atlantic. Without thinking, she reaches out, discreetly taking Marguerite's free hand with her own. Their fingers interlace beneath the cover of their skirts, hidden from prying eyes, and Marguerite gives her hand a reassuring squeeze.

Claudine looks away, eyes settling on the endless horizon. She smiles, thinking of the future stretching ahead of her, before turning back to Marguerite.

Only the woman beside her is no longer recognizable. Tattered scraps of fabric cling to what's left of her withered, blackened body. Her limbs are shrunken, her back twisted, as ash whips around her head in horrifying mockery of her silken tresses.

"Please," she begs, her voice raspy and hollow as it comes out of her lipless mouth. "You have to let this go, Claudine. Release her and let this go."

Claudine tries to let go of her hand, but Marguerite holds her in place, fingers coated in melted fat, digging into her skin. She opens her mouth and—

—gasps. Her entire body seizes forward as a fresh wave of pain pummels her. She grips the steering wheel hard, her nails pressing into the leather, a sharp breath escaping from between her lips.

Behind her, a car horn blares and she nearly jumps out of her skin.

A small queue of cars has formed behind her. Some of them are already cutting out of the lane, weaving around her in frustration. A silver car peels past, the driver leaning on their horn, their voice muffled behind closed windows as they scream something at her. A few others follow suit, honking, flipping her off as they speed past. Her face burns with shame.

She glances at the clock and her chest tightens. She's lost almost thirty minutes.

Another car honks loudly, obscenities assaulting her ears from his open window, and she presses on the gas and drives away, muttering apologies as she goes.

Ten

Jayce pulls into the driveway, slams the car into park, and rips the keys from the ignition, not bothering to lock the doors behind her. It isn't until she's halfway up the walkway that she realizes she's left her purse and phone in the vehicle.

Fuck it, she thinks, barreling toward the door door. It swings open with a loud groan, although Jayce is unsure if the sound comes from the old hinges or her lips as she stumbles across the threshold, clutching her stomach. She drops her keys as she grits her teeth against the pain, the metal clattering loudly against the wood. She throws the door closed behind her, but doesn't bother to check and see if it's actually shut.

All that matters right now is getting to the bathroom.

Another wave tears through her and it sends her to her knees, gasping as white-hot pain explodes through her lower body. *I feel like I'm being ripped in half,* she thinks, seeing stars as she crawls forward. She doesn't need to look to know she's leaving a trail behind her; she can feel it with every inch she moves. Plasma and water smear onto the floor and sweat drips off of her face. Her skirt is soaked through and clings to her body, growing wetter as more blisters burst beneath the weight of her body against the unforgiving ground. Her thighs are slick, and the evident sensation of trickling between them sends a fresh jolt of terror through her.

When she finally makes it to the bathroom, she drags herself across the cold tile and pulls herself up by the edge of the sink, her muscles trembling violently from the effort.

When she sees herself in the medicine cabinet's mirror, she hardly recognizes herself. Her skin is ghostly pale and her body looks sickly. Her skin hangs loose from her bones, sagging in unnatural folds. Her short hair is messy and drenched in sweat, sitting flat on her scalp and plastered to her face. Fluid continues to seep from the popped sores across the bridge of her nose and her lips are gouged with cracks. But the shock of the situation is momentary and her focus is quickly yanked back as the familiar roll of agony moves through her.

She wrenches open the medicine cabinet and grabs the bottle of aspirin off the shelf, popping the cap off and tilting it over. Large white pills tumble into her palm and she stuffs them greedily into her mouth, not caring if she takes too many; she's desperate and panting in pain, *anything to make this stop*. She turns on the tap, cups the water with trembling hands, and drinks deeply. She winces, only now paying attention to the soreness in her throat. She tries to think of a time today when she's had an opportunity to *stop*, to not be pulled by obligation, terror, or shielding the ones she cares for.

As another surge of cramping comes, she feels the fluid seep out from between her legs a little faster. Desperate to sit and figure out what's going on, she tucks her thumbs under the waistband of both her panties and skirt and pulls them down in a single motion.

The pain is blinding. Stars erupt from behind her eyelids and she thinks she's going to faint, her legs buckling beneath her and sending her crashing down onto the toilet. She gasps for air and her eyes sting. She looks down, her head swimming as she sees that the skin on her legs is raw and oozing. Her eyes dart to her skirt and sees small bits of translucent white stuck to the inside layer. Examining the flecks closer, and realizes with horror that the tops of her blisters must have gotten stuck on the fabric, only to be torn off with her clothing. She hangs her head between her knees, gulping down air, trying to calm herself down.

But then something inside her moves and begins to dislodge from her body. At first, it's slight, almost imperceivable, but she feels it. It's like a knot coming undone. And then, all at once, it's too much.

She cries out, her voice raw, and wraps her arms around herself. The pain is excruciating, but there's relief in it, too. She bears down, trying to push whatever it is out, but nothing happens. She gasps for breath, clutching her stomach.

This isn't normal. This isn't a period.

She can feel it moving further down as gravity pulls whatever's inside her towards its exit. And then it stops.

No. No, no, no.

Jayce holds her breath and pushes again, but it doesn't budge. She knows clots. She knows what it's like to pass them, knows the uncomfortable thickness of them, and the sensation of them slipping out. But this?

This feels different.

Solid.

Time slips and blurs as Jayce sits, folded in half, shifting uncomfortably between resting her forehead against her knees and letting her head hang between them. She's abandoned trying to sit up; each time she does, the knife in her gut twists, and she quickly buckles forward.

Time blurs together and the only indication that it's passing at all is the worsening of the pain inside of her.

Eventually, exhausted and at a standstill with the understanding that whatever's inside of her won't come out on its own, she decides to take matters into her own hands.

Spreading her legs, she reaches between them, her fingers sliding to her entrance, hesitating for only a second before pressing forward. She feels around slowly with her index finger, freezing in her tracks when she brushes against something.

It's solid.

This can't be fucking happening.

Terror rises in her throat, sharp and acidic. She tries to hook her nail into whatever it is, but it doesn't give. She swallows, and presses again, desperate to get it out. She feels resistance and takes it as a positive sign that her nail is catching before she hears a quiet squelch as it moves back inside her.

Jayce chokes on a gasp, her body going rigid.

"Fuck!" she wails, balling her free hand into a fist and slamming it against the top of her thigh in anger, not caring at the jolt of pain it sends through her.

She tries again, adjusting her approach. Jayce uses both her index and middle fingers. Slowly, carefully, she works her fingers between her walls and this *thing* inside her.

Easy does it.

She slowly wedges her finger past the blockage a millimeter at a time, and nearly sobs when she manages to find purchase. Her fingers press behind it, maneuvering it forward, easing it free with a controlled pull. And then, *finally*, it slips out.

The second it breaks loose, it drops into the water with a wet, heavy splat, the sound startling her. A mix of revulsion and relief washes over her as liquid continues to leak freely from her body. She waits nervously, holding her breath for the familiar feeling of her insides ripping apart. But it never comes.

She's so happy she could cry, and she allows herself to celebrate with tears. Under ordinary circumstances, she might have been embarrassed by the sobs of joy that wrack her body, but right now she doesn't care. Right now, in this moment, she cries in relief that the pressure inside of her is finally gone.

Once her eyes are dry, she lets out a slow exhale and reaches for some toilet paper, pausing when she notices her fingers. They're damp but otherwise clean. No blood. No streaks of pink stuck beneath her nails. In her momentary relief, she forgot; the horrible sound it made hitting the water, how she knew, deep down, this wasn't her period.

Her stomach churns.

Moving stiffly, Jayce rises from the toilet, turns, and looks down into the water.

Where a clot of blood or a clump of uterine lining should be, was instead a patch of green. Slowly, she lowers herself to the floor, her breath shallow and her pulse hammering in her ears. Her fingers grip the edge of the bowl as she leans forward, staring hard into the water as she tries to make sense of what she's looking at.

It's seaweed.

She swallows back bile and reaches into the bowl, lifting the green mass with the tips of her fingers, desperate for this to be a trick of the light, to have reality ravel itself back up. The dark, tangled leaves are unmistakable, and she reflexively lets go of her hold on the twisted ball of kelp. With a soft splash, she watches as the knotted mass of ocean flora sinks to the bottom of the bowl.

"What the fuck? *What the fuck? WHAT THE FUCK?!*" Her voice rises with each repetition, the panic setting it. As she backs away from the toilet, she feels it.

Something wet brushing against her thigh.

Her stomach lurches.

She can't bring herself to look down and so she feels around, her hands trembling as they skim across her inner thigh, her fingers eventually finding the slippery wet rope of seaweed that hangs half out of her body.

She lets out a strangled scream and pulls at it, desperately tearing it from her body. It comes free with little resistance. The green strands slither out of her, spilling wetly onto the bathroom tiles, splattering clear fluid across the floor, and landing cold against her bare feet. The smell hits her hard—the unmistakable brine of the ocean—and Jayce dry heaves. She runs her hands frantically between her legs, slipping her fingers between her folds, checking for any remnants of seaweed. She runs her hands along her thighs and she pauses as they pass over the unmistakable grit of sand that peppers her skin.

Her shoulders sag forward and her body trembles. And then, finally, she breaks. Tears spill freely down her cheeks, her breath breaking in ragged gasps.

What the fuck is happening to me?

She closes her eyes—

—and cries quietly.

"Shhhh. It's okay. It's all going to be okay" Marguerite murmurs, winding her arms around Claudine and drawing her close. Claudine sniffles, pressing her forehead against the other woman's and finding comfort in the gentle way Marguerite tucks a strand of hair behind her ear.

She exhales shakily, blinking away the wetness in her eyes.

Marguerite tilts her chin up towards her, and their lips meet in a slow, lingering kiss.

"It's going to be okay," Marguerite whispers against her mouth.

Claudine doesn't know if it's the reassurance or the raw ache of it all, but something inside her shatters, and the tears come faster.

This isn't right. This isn't supposed to be happening.

She chokes on the words, her voice breaking as she speaks. "He can't do this to you."

Marguerite lets out a sad laugh. "Life's not fair. Isn't that what they say?"

Claudine clenches her jaw.

"He can't do this to you," she repeats. She says the words more forceful this time, as if her sheer will alone can make it true.

Marguerite flinches at the anger in Claudine's voice, but remains quiet. The truth of the matter is that Marguerite's father can do this.

Has *done this.*

"Honestly," she says, "I should be thankful that he didn't send me away the moment he heard of François' passing. And how can he be expected to turn up his nose at this offer? To have my dowry paid? To give me what he thinks is a chance at a better life? I shouldn't be so ungrateful."

"Marguerite—"

"My father needs me to do this. My family needs me to do this."

Claudine stares at her, voice hoarse as she asks, "And what about what I need?" When Marguerite doesn't answer, Claudine's hands ball into fists. "Do I not matter to you? Do my needs count for nothing?"

Marguerite's expression cracks, a flash of something raw and painful breaks through the surface, but she shoves it back down and out of sight before she answers. "The sooner I accept it," she murmurs, "the sooner we can make the most of the time we have left."

"And if I don't want to say goodbye?" The words slip out before Claudine can hold them back and hide them somewhere where they won't hurt so much.

"It's already been decided."

Silence swells between them, thick and suffocating.

"I can't stop you from going," Claudine finally says, meeting Marguerite's gaze. "But that doesn't mean I can't go with you."

"What?" she asks, her breath hitching at the back of her throat.

"I'll go with you. I'll petition my father to let me go with you."

Marguerite's lips part in what Claudine thinks is shock, but then she sees her expression for what it really is.

Hope.

Dangerous, fragile, impossible hope.

Marguerite trembles. "Claudine, I can't ask you to do that."

"You're not asking," Claudine whispers, taking the other woman's hands in her own. "Because where my heart goes, my body follows."

The words echo—

—around the small room. Jayce blinks slowly as she looks around, taking in her surroundings, and remembering herself once more.

The bathroom tiles are cold against her naked skin and she shivers hard, wrapping her arms around herself and wishing they were Bridget's.

Eleven

Jayce abandons her attempt to clean the bathroom shortly after she starts it. She manages to gather the ropes of seaweed and mop up some of the water, but the effort quickly becomes futile. Liquid continues to dribble out from between her legs and the blisters ooze saltwater. The discharge from them dries on her skin, leaving familiar patches of salt on her clothes. And to make matters worse, the older pustules have begun to leak something new: sand and seafoam. Small streams of foamy grit push through her skin, tumbling to the floor in wet, muddy heaps. Her throat continues to burn. The dull ache that had been creeping up since the morning is now a raging fire, her tonsils swollen and raw, flecks of white peeking out from their crypts. Her mouth is both too dry and too wet, her saliva tinged with the taste of salt and the texture of sand. The cramps in her abdomen have eased, but that's only made way for a new pain to crop up: a faint discomfort that radiates from her shoulder, the muscle bulging against her skin, coiling tight and seizing whenever she turns her neck.

Despite the fear that grips her, a single thought makes its way to the forefront of her mind: Le Saint-Clément.

She shivers uncontrollably as she types the name of the ship into the search bar, her bandage-wrapped fingers stiff and clumsy. Her eyes scan through the results, barely registering them as the disposable pads layered between her legs grow heavy with the endless amount of seawater that pours out of her body. She debates trying to adjust them in the hopes of making herself more comfortable, but knows it's a losing battle. In addition to the two pads she's fixed to a pair of reusable period panties, Jayce is covered in tight layers packed thick with cloth in an attempt to slow the oozing of her blisters. She used up the last of the gauze, bandages, and even the paper towels, before resorting to packing folded-up facecloths and dish towels under layers of compression gear she normally reserved for working out. She can smell herself; pungent and salty.

She shakes her head and focuses on the web results, hoping that this search is at least a bit more fruitful than her other ones have been. To no one's surprise, online health sites couldn't offer her a reasonable diagnosis for the saltwater and seaweed being expelled from her body, and a general search was predictably useless when she looked for Claudine and Marguerite, her search for them yielding nothing but frustration.

Thankfully, her research on the ship is proving to be a little more successful, although what little she uncovers only raises more questions. The Le Saint-Clément was a real ship. It carried soldiers, supplies, and women—known as *Les Filles du Roi*, who were sent by order of the king with dowries paid and promises of marriage—to Nouvelle-France. But beyond that, the ship's fate is unknown.

Her fists clench, the bandages stretching tight across her open skin. Her body is falling apart, and she's no closer to understanding things now than she was this morning. The screen blurs, tears burning behind her eyes.

"Jayce!" Bridget calls, her voice loud and panicked. "Jayce! Are you here?"

She jumps in her seat, her partner's voice catching her off guard., and her chair scrapes against the floor as she spins toward the bedroom door.

Bridget stands in the hallway, her eyes wide, mouth open. Horrified.

Her gaze follows the wet trail to the waterlogged bathroom, past clusters of sand and seafoam, and finally lands on Jayce. She takes in the sight of her partner wrapped tightly, blistered, and pale, and covers her mouth with trembling hands.

"Oh my God," Bridget gasps, rushing forward to Jayce. She extends her arms to hold her but stops herself from making contact as she stares at the painful welts. Instead, she gently tilts Jayce's head upwards. "What the fuck happened?"

"They got worse," Jayce whispers, her voice cracking as Bridget's eyes track the fresh blisters that have multiplied across Jayce's skin like an infection, as if the ocean itself is consuming her. Her eyes take in the deflated folds of flesh that hang from her beautiful face, the pain that radiates from her eyes, and Bridget's heart breaks for Jayce.

"You need to go to the hospital."

Jayce's gaze drifts past Bridget to the window, noticing for the first time just how dark the sky has gotten. "You're home early."

"I am," she snaps. "I was fucking worried about you. I tried calling you, but you never picked up. And then I texted you, but I got nothing. So I called the coffee house and River told me you left early because you got sick! So, yeah, I'm home early!" Her voice cracks with panic. "Jesus, Jayce. You *promised* you'd call if it got worse."

"I'm sorry. I didn't mean to scare you."

"I don't care that you scared me! I care that you're sick! You need to see a doctor, babe."

Jayce shakes her head weakly, her voice hoarse. "They can't help me."

"It's a *hospital*, Jayce. I think they know more about this than you do."

"Do you think they can diagnose why I pulled *seaweed out of my pussy*, Bridget?" she asks, voice rising.

"*What?*"

"Yeah, fucking seaweed in my goddamn pussy. That was a new one."

"There has to be a reason for it. I mean, it can't just... it doesn't just... Maybe it happened when we fooled around?" Bridget says, desperately trying to make sense of the situation.

"Unless you finger blasted an entire coil of seaweed into me—which I think at least one of us would have noticed—then I doubt it." she says, voice shaking. "But, hey, maybe you're right! If they can't solve the mystery of my *Aquaticus Vaginous*, maybe they'll at least be able to tell me why I'm seeing shit."

"Like what, babe?" Bridget asks softly.

"I keep seeing you," she admits, her voice small. "But it's not *you* you. It's you on fire."

Bridget freezes, her voice softening. "Jayce..."

Jayce's throat burns, her voice ragged as she breaks, "I'm hallucinating *you*. I see you burning. I smell it. And I know it's not real but—"

Bridget lets go of Jayce's face and sinks to her knees, resting her hands delicately on Jayce's thighs, who recoils at the touch. Bridget stares at her with melted eyes, plumes of smoke rising from her charred scalp, her skin peeling back in sheets. She rubs her thumb absentmindedly against Jayce's black leggings, smearing a trail of ash on the black spandex.

"Tell me, babe, what's going on in that head of yours?" she asks, her voice delicate and steady despite it all.

"Nothing," she lies, her voice barely above a whisper. "It's nothing."

And Bridget—*beautiful, burning Bridget*—cups her chin again. "You promised you'd go if it got worse. And this..." her voice cracks. "This is *worse*, Jayce."

"We both know they can't fix this." The full force of this admission cracks something inside her.

"We don't know that. But if they can't fix you, they can at least help you. So please, *please*, just go," Bridget pleads.

Jayce's throat is dry with salt and her chest is tight from the conversation. A bead of the ocean itself drips from a bandage across her nose and lands on her bottom lip, stinging the cracks in her skin.

"Okay," she rasps, finally giving in. "I'll go tomorrow. First thing."

"Okay," Bridget whispers back. "First thing."

Twelve

Before the sun has even set, Jayce lets Bridget lead her to bed. She covers her in warm blankets and soft kisses before settling next to Jayce, wrapping her arms around her, and holding her close. Despite the layers of fleece, Jayce's body continues to shake violently from the cold that grows inside of her.

The two of them lie in silence and Jayce closes her eyes finding refuge in the warmth of Bridget's arms—

—when she's suddenly overcome with a fresh wave of nausea. Claudine rolls onto her side, her face hanging over the edge of the bed as cold sweat drips to the floor. She heaves, her stomach clenching, her mind blank as her body tries once more to purge itself. She aims for the metal bucket below, but knows she doesn't need to; like last time, nothing comes out.

She coughs, her throat raw and burning as she collapses back onto the mattress. Marguerite rolls her gently onto her side, finds the small of Claudine's back, and rubs small circles into it, her voice soft as she whispers words of reassurance and comfort. Another wave of nausea crashes into Claudine, and she bolts up to dry heave over the side of the bed once more.

"I wish there was a physician aboard," Marguerite says when Claudine finally stills.

"I'm fine," Claudine rasps, her voice so hoarse it betrays the lie.

"You're not." Marguerite's brows knit together, her worry unmistakable. "You're ill."

"I'm not ill," Claudine protests. "I'm sick from all the rocking. I wasn't made for the water."

Marguerite shifts closer, her body pressing against Claudine's as she wraps a protective arm around her waist, her grip solid but loose enough for her to break away if another wave hits. "I'm still worried," she murmurs.

"I know. But you don't have to be," Claudine promises.

She knows Marguerite's fear isn't without cause. Of the eight women who set sail from France, four have already died as victims of an unknown illness sweeping through the ship. Two of the deckhands have already succumbed, and a third's wet, hacking cough reverberates throughout the ship, audible no matter where you are on board. Provisions—which were spread thin to begin with—are now running low while the harsh seas and stubborn winds stretch their voyage longer than it should be.

Marguerite stays by her side, brushing damp strands of hair from Claudine's forehead, her fingers soft as they trace her skin. After every heave, she kisses Claudine's temple and whispers comforting words in her ear, her warm breath sending shivers down Claudine's spine.

Eventually, the heaves subside, leaving Claudine weak and trembling but no longer at war with her stomach.

"You should go back to your quarters," she murmurs, her lips brushing Marguerite's palm.

"Why should I?" Marguerite's voice is firm. "Let them find me. There's nothing indecent about me caring for you, especially when you don't have the strength to do it yourself. Even they'd have to realize that."

Claudine laughs at Marguerite's defiance.

"I love you." The words slip out before she can stop them. Although she means what she says, this isn't how she'd imagined confessing her love for the first time; sweat-drenched and nauseated. Marguerite stills and Claudine fears she's said too much, her mind suddenly racing on ways to fix her mistake.

But then Marguerite leans in and presses her lips against Claudine's, the kiss delicate and unhurried.

"I love you too," she whispers.

Their lips meet once more and this time, the kiss is brimming with need and hunger. Claudine revels in the taste of the other woman, the warmth of her touch, the smell of her sweat, until her exhaustion eventually wins out and forces her to rest once more. Marguerite settles down on the bed behind her, her arms holding Claudine tight, their bodies fitting together as though they were always meant to.

The ship groans, waves slamming hard against its hull, and Claudine's heavy eyelids flutter open—

—surprised by how cold she suddenly feels. Jayce looks around, confused, as she tries to piece her current situation together.

When she'd fallen asleep, it was curled up with Bridget in the warmth of their bed. But now, the frigid water laps at her knees and she trembles, her body ravaged and aching.

How did I get here?

She's still dressed in the compression set she fell asleep in, fabric clinging to her leaking wounds. She glances back towards the beach, her eyes scanning the sand dunes and empty expanse of road for her car, but her search comes up empty. She realizes that she must have walked here, lured from her bed to the sea.

She wants to turn back and run from the freezing tide, but something deep within her prevents her from going back and urges her forward. She doesn't want to, but she takes a step forward anyway. The cold numbs her skin and makes it hard to think.

Just a little more, something whispers from inside her. *Just a little more and we can go home.*

"Home," Jayce says, the word sweet on her lips. She closes her eyes, struggling to picture it, when a sudden image flashes through her mind: Bridget.

She smiles as she pictures her partner's face, beautiful and familiar. She remembers her strong arms, that have only ever held her close, and her warm hands, that have only ever touched her with love. She can hear Bridget's voice in the back of her mind, thick with good humour and kind words, and she imagines her bright eyes. Jayce can't help but wonder if they'd still light up like that if she suddenly vanished into the ocean. Would she still be able to smile, or would that be lost with Jayce? Would she know that this wasn't a choice Jayce made for herself, or would she think she was abandoned?

When she imagines Bridget's heartbreak, the pain in Jayce's chest becomes unbearable. And so, with every ounce of strength she has left, Jayce turns back and heads towards the shore. Every step forward is agony, as though she's ripping herself from the ocean's grasp. Her body fights her, heavy and sluggish, but she refuses to give up. The ocean churns around her in anger at her defiance, calling home what's pouring out of her flesh. She never lets Bridget's face leave her mind's eye as she finally reaches the sand and her legs give out. She collapses onto her chest, the sand rough against her cheek, and exhaustion holds her down and stops her from moving. She gasps for air, each breath thick and laboured, and her eyes eventually flutter closed, the taste of salt coating her tongue—

—as she screams, her voice lost in the waves.

Pressure crushes Claudine from all sides, squeezing her bones, and expelling the last of her breath from her lips. She fights against the water, desperate for the surface and to return to Marguerite.

She holds her breath for as long as she can but, eventually, her body betrays her and desperately attempts to gulp air in. Instead, saltwater floods her lungs and sets her nerves on fire. She thrashes against the icy current, but it's hopeless with her limbs bound together and the sea's crushing weight.

She looks up, and an orange glow dances on the waves, illuminating Le Saint-Clément's name on the stern as she slips deeper into the ocean. Black begins to creep in at the edges of her vision, the light overhead slowly dimming.

Please. Please, God, *she thinks.* Help her. Please, help her. Punish me, but have mercy on her. Please, save her. Please… I have to save her. *Claudine begs.*

But she knows it's hopeless: her words won't find Him from this deep in the ocean.

The pain is blinding, but it soon begins to fade as the cold numbs her body. She doesn't want to die, but she's grateful for the relief it brings.

As the waves swallow her up and the last of the light fades away, she hears the voice.

"Please, my love," Marguerite begs. "You need to let go. You need to let us go."

Claudine's eyes shoot open and—

Thirteen

—It takes Jayce a moment to realize what she's looking at. The edges of her vision are bruised, black and blue, as if the water seeping from her body is clouding her eyes. She realizes with a start that she's no longer on the beach, but she hasn't returned home either.

Instead, she stands in front of the locked doors to the Centre Culturel Des Îles-de-la-Madeleine, a museum dedicated to the founding of Les Îles and the settling of Quebec.

"Why am I here?"

A name flashes through her mind as if answering her.

"Le Saint-Clément," she says, her voice hoarse and brittle. "Is that what you brought me here to see?" she asks. She desperately wants to go back home to be with Bridget, but her body itches and weeps for something behind those glass doors.

The sign in the window says the museum only opens up at noon. The sky is dark overhead and given how much thinner her body feels and how frail she's become, she doubts she'll live long enough to see the dawn, let alone their opening hours.

Better to ask for forgiveness, she thinks.

She picks up one of the heavy planters and struggles to lift it overhead, the rough stone scraping her sensitive skin, before slamming it hard against the glass door, easily shattering it. As she steps over the broken glass, a few of the shards biting into her feet, she wonders if her intrusion has set off a silent alarm. A small part of her hopes that it has so that she won't be alone when she fades into nothingness.

Her body moves through the museum, knowing where it's going even if she doesn't. Each step sends a fresh wave of pain shooting through her, the glass crunching against bone with each step. She knows she should be surprised when she looks back at the trail of footprints she's leaving and sees only pools of water—not blood—in her wake, but she isn't. She knows deep within her, that something cold and coiled, has changed the rules. She coughs, her lungs sore and heavy as she ascends the stairs to the second floor.

Something hard presses against the back of her throat and she wiggles her tongue, trying to figure out what it is through touch alone. Her cold, damp hands palpate her neck, fingers pressing around her jawbone and beneath her chin, remembering the tonsil stones she'd seen forming earlier in the day. Desperate for relief, she presses her skin hard, she feels a pop as something hard jets through the skin of her throat. It hurts—*everything* hurts—but the sudden release from the pressure brings a nearly orgasmic sense of relief.

She wiggles her tongue again. The rough patch at the back of her mouth is more pronounced and fills the space with a familiar, sandpaper-like texture. She spots a sign for the washroom ahead, but her body takes her down another hallway: one that leads toward the exhibit on the settlers of Nouvelle-France.

Confused, she scans the display, searching for any mention of *Le Saint-Clément* but finds none. She reads the placards, trusting her legs wouldn't have brought her here without reason. The museum notes that while the colonies of Nouvelle-France had fewer pirate encounters than others, the cold Atlantic was not without its dangers.

She grows bored with the display of burly pirates and pop-culture inaccuracies but keeps reading. Just as she's ready to move on, a small section about the settlement of Quebec catches her eye, her pulse quickening when she spots the words "Le Saint-Clément" on a placard detailing the ship's ill-fated journey.

Departing Dieppe in 1664 with a full crew and eight of the Filles du Roi, the mercantile ship, Le Saint-Clément, never reached Quebec. Although a manifest could never be recovered from the shipwreck, historians believe that shortages from the war and rampant illness had plagued the voyage, and turbulent weather likely forced the crew to navigate choppy waters on meager rations.

Beside the sign are large photos of the ship as it rests on the ocean floor. The wood is splintered and rotted, coral growing off of its broken bow, planks of wood buried in the sand, the anchor rusted brown.

She reads the next placard.

Though deep-sea excursions have recovered the wreckage, initial theories of a storm or navigational error proved unlikely. Close examination of the debris revealed extensive fire damage most often seen in vessels recovered after battle. Many historians believe the Le Saint-Clément fell prey to pirates, likely driven by economic necessity rather than greed.

A knot forms in her stomach. The story doesn't sit right.

"You knew them," Jayce whispers, remembering how she recognized the faces of the men. "Pirates? That doesn't make sense."

She moves on, grateful the section is ending but feeling no closer to understanding than she did before she arrived. She reads the last of the signs. This one is mounted on the wall behind a sheet of glass, a row of half-preserved objects arranged in a row neatly beside it.

Although there was little remaining in the wreckage of Le Saint-Clément upon its discovery, divers were able to salvage a few preserved goods including a trunk, weaponry, and even a few bottles of wine.

As she passes the display, a flash of purple catches her eye. She leans closer, pressing a hand to the glass, saltwater dripping from her fingers and pooling on the floor below. She stares at the handkerchief, her throat tightening as she admires it. Although the cream linen is now yellowed, the faded bouquets of violas still show through the grime.

"Marguerite," she coos, voice cracking. The name spills from her lips with a pang of longing, and she aches with memory. Her body weeps for Marguerite's soft hands, the taste of tart apples and honey that drips from her lips, and the warmth of her body. She opens her mouth to call for Marguerite once more but stops as she remembers herself.

"Bridget," she whispers.

Her body is suddenly heavy with shame. How could she pine for anyone else or miss the touch of a woman she'd never even met?

Nausea twists her stomach and she stumbles through the museum, back the way she came, desperately searching for the washroom she'd passed only moments ago.

She crashes through the door and reaches the sink just in time, her body heaving. Liquid forces its way violently up her throat, the bitter saltwater pouring from her lips and splattering against the porcelain. Then, something solid tumbles out. She coughs, again, and again, and again, until the sink is lined with wet sand. Something moves beneath the surface and Jayce realizes with horror that a handful of tiny crabs scuttle through the mud. A new wave of nausea hits her, and this time the retching brings even more crabs. Dozens of them spill from her lips, each one no bigger than a nickel, and scurry around the sink, trying—and failing—to climb up the slippery walls. A few of them cling to her shirt, their little claws pinching her skin, their legs kicking as they hang dangerously high in the air. When she finally stops, she musters up enough courage to look at herself in the mirror.

The woman staring back at her is a stranger. Her hollow eyes, sunken cheeks, and ghostly pale skin with dark blue veins visible beneath her near-translucent flesh are nothing like the way she remembers herself from only a day ago.

She coughs once more, expelling a glob of sand, and feels something sharp still lodged in the back of her throat. She opens her mouth and inspects her tonsils in the mirror, wondering if it's a crab hanging onto her body for dear life.

It's not.

Barnacles cover her tonsils, spread along the back of her throat, and have begun coating the inside of her cheeks.

Between the blistered skin, her shrinking body, and the way her mind is slowly going, she knows her time is short. Without wasting another minute, she leaves the museum and heads home.

Fourteen

ALTHOUGH JAYCE MARCHES TOWARDS HER HOUSE, HER BODY REFUSES to take her there. She walks slowly, trying to head down the main road while her legs bring her closer to the water's edge.

She wants to go home and find refuge one last time in Bridget's arms before her body unravels and Jayce slips away.

Please. I don't want to die alone.

Despite her struggle, her body is unrelenting and drags her unwillingly toward the beach.

"Jayce?" a familiar voice calls out behind her.

"Bridget?" she asks, voice hardly a whisper.

Jayce makes her way to the shoulder of the road, stumbles over a small cement island, and begins her march across the sand, the ocean creeping ever closer. Behind her on the main road, a car speeds up, turns on its high beams, and illuminates Jayce's steady crawl to the water.

"Jayce? *Jayce?*" Bridget screams louder this time. "Jayce, what are you doing?"

Although Jayce can't stop herself from moving forward, she whips her head wildly around, desperate to see Bridget one last time. Her partner sits behind the steering wheel, eyes wide with panic, her long hair disheveled. She's still in her pajamas, not having bothered to change before rushing out in search of Jayce.

"Please, you're scaring me!" she cries. "Where are you going?"

"I'm sorry," Jayce shouts back, her voice breaking. She knows her words won't make any sense, but she needs Bridget to know this isn't a choice she's making for herself. "I don't want to go, but I can't stop! She won't let me!"

"Please, Jayce! Just come home!" Bridget screams desperately.

"I can't!" Jayce sobs, shoulders heaving. "I want to, but I can't."

Her voice is rough and broken, the rough barnacles cutting her tongue and scratching against her teeth as she speaks, new clusters of them growing on the roof of her mouth and in the space between her lips and gums. She stumbles down the last few feet of the sand dune, the ocean mist chilling her skin.

She wants to be brave, but she isn't, and tears fall freely as her body forces her closer to the water.

Jayce turns and looks back at Bridget, too terrified to look out into the water, her neck and shoulders screaming in protest. Bridget has pulled the car onto the sand dune, the driver's side door flung open, the engine still purring. Bridget, however, barrels towards Jayce, her bare feet slipping on the sand as she rushes to her side.

"Jayce, stop!" she pleads. "You have to stop! I'm begging you!"

"It's not me!" Jayce tries to explain, her voice cracking with terror. "I can't stop! Please, I want to, but I can't!"

Bridget throws out an arm to pull her away from the water, her fingers clutching Jayce's sore shoulder. When she pulls back, the skin sloughs off as easily as wet paper, the fabric of her shirt crumbling at Bridget's touch as if rotted through, and water seeps from the open wound. Bridget screams in shock, the clump of flesh in her hand bubbling as it melts away into sea foam. Both women stare, their eyes wide and transfixed, as something writhes where Jayce's muscle should be. An eel squirms through the torn flesh, slithering free and landing on the sand, wriggling and desperate for the water.

Jayce takes another step forward, the ice-cold ocean pooling around her ankles. "What's happening to me?" she sobs, terror choking her voice as she's dragged forward again, the water now coming to her knees.

Before she can take another step, Bridget's arms wrap around her, holding her tightly. She presses her body against Jayce's back, trying to anchor her to the shore without breaking more of her partner's body. She trembles, and Jayce swears she can feel Bridget's pulse, fast and frantic, through her skin.

"It's okay," Bridget whispers, her voice shaking. "It's gonna be okay. I'm here. I've got you."

"I'm scared," Jayce cries, her body fighting against Bridget's grip as it drags itself deeper into the sea.

"I've got you," she says again.

Jayce closes her eyes, her breathing ragged, and savors the warmth of Bridget's skin against her own for what may be the last time.

"I love you,"—

—Claudine whispers, her lips brushing against Marguerite's ear.

"I love you, too," Marguerite replies, her breath hot on Claudine's neck. They kiss deeply, savoring each other. Claudine tightens her lips around Marguerite's retreating tongue, their connection electric.

Marguerite's hands glide up Claudine's back, fingers threading into her hair, nails scraping gently against her scalp. Goosebumps rise on Claudine's skin, and she moans softly. Marguerite's lips travel down her neck, chest, and shoulders. Her hand moves against Claudine's breast, brushing her thumb over the hardening nipple. Claudine gasps, her pulse quickening as Marguerite's touch grows more insistent.

Claudine straddles Marguerite's leg, her hips moving on their own as she grinds down against her lover. She gasps as Marguerite presses her thigh up against her, deepening the sensation. She can feel herself growing wetter and she knows she's making a mess of the other woman's nightgown; a fact that only brings her closer to the edge. The fabric sticking to her thigh.

She closes her eyes, enjoying the warmth of Marguerite's breath against her neck as the two of them pant softly. The fabric of her nightgown is slicked wet and sticks to the other woman's thigh, the white cotton turned translucent. Waves break against the hull, the ship creaking and groaning from the impact.

Her breath hitches in her throat and her heart beats like a war drum, her body moving in rhythm with her lover and the sea as she rubs herself against the thigh that's been positioned between her legs. She runs her fingers through the thick curls gathered at the nape of the other woman's neck, her hair ribbon loosening and falling to the floor.

"I love you," she whispers.

"I love you, too," Marguerite moans.

The heat between her thighs is unbearable as it breaks. She bites her lip to keep from crying out, her body trembling, clinging onto Marguerite for dear life as she rides her climax out, stars bursting at the edges of her vision. When it finally ends, she slumps against Marguerite, catching her breath before cupping the other woman's face and peppering small kisses across her skin.

Marguerite smiles, her eyes alight in the darkness, hungry for more.

Before either of them knows what's happening, the door to the cabin bursts open. Strong hands grab Claudine, ripping her off of Marguerite and throwing her hard against the floor, pain shooting through her. The hands grab at her again, lifting her onto her feet and dragging her out of the small room. She fights back against the man, trying to free herself of his grip, pulling her shoulder painfully in the process as she flails against him.

Behind her in the small room, Marguerite screams for them to let Claudine go.

"We knew this was more than ill fortune," the man shouts, his face red and veins bulging with rage. "But none of us could figure out what we'd done to incur God's wrath like this. But we should have known it was one of you. You're why this is happening to us. You're the reason good men have died." Spit flies from his lips, hitting her face as he yells.

Claudine recoils in fear as they pull her towards the stairs, waves—

—crash against Jayce's body as she struggles, Claudine's will driving her forward into the Atlantic. Bridget fights desperately to hold Jayce back, her grip fierce, but they both know her strength means nothing against the ocean itself.

"Please," Jayce sobs, voice breaking, "don't let the sea take me."

"I've got you!" Bridget shouts, refusing to let go.

Jayce wails, terrified of what's waiting for her beneath the surface, her body aching—

—as her leg hits the side of the stair. Claudine struggles for purchase, trying to get her feet underneath her as she's dragged up the wet wooden steps.

The ship creaks, water slamming against the hull, sea foam spraying high into the air and soaking through the thin linen of her nightgown. Below deck, she can hear Marguerite yelling and struggling against another person as they attempt to drag her upstairs too. Claudine stumbles, falling forward, but strong arms lift her before she can hit the ground, dragging her up onto the deck of the ship.

A group of men stand clustered together, and although their expressions range from quiet rage to blistering hate, they all have one thing in common: eyes gleaming with violent intent. Had Claudine not spent the last few weeks aboard the ship with them, she wouldn't have been able to recognize them as members of the crew. She opens her mouth to plead for help, but the wind is knocked out of her before she gets a chance as she's thrown hard to the ground, seawater splashing around her. She shivers and gasps for air, her body shaking.

One of the men leans over and grabs her hands roughly.

"Stop! Get off of me!" Claudine tries to pull away, but his grip only tightens, her bones threatening to snap beneath his tremendous strength. She continues to shout as a rough length cord is wrapped excruciatingly taut around her wrists before another man grabs her legs and binds her ankles.

She writhes on the ground, struggling against her bonds as the men yell and spit at her. Somewhere behind her, she can hear Marguerite pleading with someone to let Claudine go.

"We shouldn't have taken them aboard," one of them says.

"I told you it was bad luck to sail with women," says another.

"They're cursed!" someone shouts.

"We're being tested!" another chimes in.

An oil lamp clutched in one man's hands flickers, painting the faces of the mob in deep, ever-shifting reds. "We are being judged for their sins," he says. "If we want to make it to port, we need to atone. And they need to be punished."

Marguerite is thrown onto the deck beside her. Before the men can tie her feet, she kicks out, struggling wildly against them, and they give her space like they would any other cornered animal. A few of them laugh and pretend to lunge at her, clearly enjoying the panic in her eyes. Claudine watches as the ring of men around Marguerite gets a little smaller, their eyes alight with rage. Her heart, already pounding, threatens to burst.

"No!" Claudine shouts. "She didn't do anything! It was me! Me alone! I seduced her! Please! I'm the only one that deserves to be punished! Please!"

"You're right," a man beside her hisses. She recognizes him; his face had been

kind and gentle when he had helped her aboard the ship. It was nothing like that now. "You do deserve to be punished." He grabs the front of her nightgown, hoisting her up.

"Please!" Marguerite cries. "Have mercy!"

Claudine struggles against the man as he drags her toward the edge of the ship.

"No! Please don't!" she screams, her voice catching in her throat as he lifts her off the ground, her legs banging against the ship's railing. The ocean churns below her, the water black and unforgiving, and Claudine is filled so full of terror that she can't find it in her to feel shame as a trail of wet warmth runs down her thigh. "No! Please! No!" she cries.

"Claudine!" Marguerite yells, her voice a wail of despair as the men close in, ropes in hand.

Claudine breathes fast, bile rising in the back of her throat she looks down.

Behind her, someone screams, and Claudine's eyes widen in horror as she takes in the sight before her.

A fire has broken out on the deck of the ship. The oil lantern that was once held by one of the crewmen now lies broken in pieces at his feet, his body engulfed in flames that cast eerie shadows against the sails in the dead of the night. He panics, flailing desperately as he tries to put himself out, but instead only helps to quicken the spread of the blaze.

But it's not the burning boat that Claudine notices. Instead, her eyes are glued to Marguerite who locks eyes with her one final time before agony splits her face, mouth stretched wide in a desperate scream as her gown burns hot against her skin, her long hair catching fire.

Claudine screams, desperate to put out the fire that burns Marguerite alive, the air heavy with the stench of burning flesh and bubbling fat. She rallies against the hands that hold her, desperate to save her partner, but it's pointless.

She can't even save herself.

With a final heave, the man pushes Claudine over the edge of the ship, her body free-falling before slamming into the water below. The air is knocked from her lungs as she screams, her voice lost in the waves.

Pressure crushes Claudine from all sides, squeezing her bones, and expelling the last of her breath from her lips. She fights against the water, desperate for the surface and to return to Marguerite.

She holds her breath for as long as she can but, eventually, her body betrays her and desperately attempts to gulp air in. Instead, saltwater floods her lungs and sets her nerves on fire. She thrashes against the icy current, but it's hopeless with her limbs bound together and the sea's crushing weight.

She looks up, and an orange glow dances on the waves, illuminating Le Saint-Clément's name on the stern as she slips deeper into the ocean. Black begins to creep in at the edges of her vision, the light overhead slowly dimming.

Please. Please, God, *she thinks.* Help her. Please, help her. Punish me, but have mercy on her. Please, save her. Please… I have to save her. *Claudine begs.*

But she knows it's hopeless: her words won't find Him from this deep in the ocean.

The pain is blinding, but it soon begins to fade as the cold numbs her body. She doesn't want to die, but she's grateful for the relief it brings.—

—Claudine drives Jayce deeper into the sea, the water already up past her waist. With every step forward, Jayce knows that Bridget's chances of getting out of the water alive diminish, the tide dangerously high and the current deathly strong.

"I'm sorry," she tells Bridget, her voice breaking. "I'm sorry that I won't get to see you start your new job. I'm sorry that I won't get to marry you, that I won't get to grow old with you. I'm sorry for every time I didn't do the laundry, or didn't listen, or went to bed angry. I'm sorry for every time I wanted to say 'I love you,' but was too nervous to tell you, so I didn't," she sobs, the words pouring out from her lips all at once.

Bridget grips her and she screams, muscles shaking as she tries to pull Jayce towards the shore. She's fighting with everything she has, but Jayce knows it's no use as she takes another step forward.

"I love you," Jayce tells her frantically. "And I'll always love you, even if I'm not there to tell you. I'll always love you."

Bridget can't hold back her tears any longer. She lets herself sob alongside Jayce, breathless and gasping for air as she fights against her partner's body that moves forward of its own volition.

"I love you too," Bridget cries between shaking breaths, "but I'm not gonna let you go like this."

"You have to," Jayce tells her, the water nearly up past her ribs. "If you don't, it'll take you too. The current's too strong. You have to let me go."

"I won't. I can't."

She continues to pull Jayce towards the beach, but it's clear that this is a losing battle. Jayce's body shakes, ice-cold fear runs down her spine and an exhaustion that only comes when defeat sets in.

"Let me go," she croaks. "Please, you have to let me go."

Before Bridget can argue, a pair of hands reach down towards the two women huddled together in the waves. They're long and thin, the choppy waters visible through their translucent skin. Jayce looks up and sees a face familiar to her only in memory.

Marguerite looks through her, her hands reaching forward as if to cup her face but instead they pass into her, sinking deep into her skin, gently tilting Claudine's face up towards hers, the woman's form shimmering atop Jayce's as if her image had been superimposed.

"You have to let this go, Claudine," she says sadly. "You have to let us go."

Claudine cries and tries to pull away from Marguerite, but the woman holds her in place.

"I can't," she sobs. "I have to save you. And I can! This time, I can do it."

Marguerite smiles sadly at her. "No matter how many times you try to save me, Claudine. You never will," Marguerite says firmly. "No matter how many vessels you inhabit, no matter how many people you bring to the water, you can never save me. I'm already gone. We both are."

Claudine pulls away, shaking her head violently from side to side. "I need to do this.

I need to get to you. I can save you!" Claudine shouts, heartbroken. "If I can just put out the fire, we can be together again. I can hold you again. Please, I can save you."

"You can't. You'll always be too late, but that's okay," Marguerite tells her, leaning down to tuck a strand of hair behind Claudine's ear, lifting her spirit out of Jayce a little more. "You'll always be too late, Claudine. You'll never be able to stop the fire, because no matter how many times you rally against the past, it's already happened. We can't change it. We can only move forward."

"I can't!" she yells. "I want to, but I can't!"

"Please, Claudine. Don't take away their chance to have what we did," Marguerite says, looking sadly at Jayce and Bridget.

"What we had?" she yells. "We were supposed to be together! To start our lives together! And it was taken away in an instant! I won't let our future slip through my fingers. Not again. How can you ask me to give us up?"

"I would never ask that of you. *Never*. But how is this a future for either of us when you keep forcing us to relive these past torments? But the longer you hold onto this pain—the longer you try to change the past—the longer you keep us apart. We're already gone, my love. So why are you fighting so hard for us to stay?"

"If it's torment, then why are you still here?" she asks. "Why won't you move on?"

Marguerite smiles. "That's easy: because where my heart goes, my body follows."

It takes a second for the words to register, but when they do, Claudine's face crumples into tears. She throws her arms around Marguerite and sobs against her, letting herself be pulled gently from Jayce's body.

"I'm sorry," she whispers to Marguerite. "I'm so sorry."

In the water, Jayce collapses against Bridget. She's exhausted and in pain, but the relief at being free once more overwhelms her, and she can't stop the great heaving sobs that escape her.

Bridget tightens her grip around Jayce and begins pulling her— this time successfully—towards the shore. "I've got you," she says, pressing small kisses against her partner's skin. "I've got you and I won't let you go."

As the sun begins to crest over the horizon, painting the water in soft orange light.

"Let's go home," Marguerite says, gently squeezing Claudine's hand.

The other woman nods, smiling through her tears. Bridget and

Jayce watch, transfixed, as the two women slowly dissolve into seafoam, scattering into the waves.

The current continues to tug at Bridget and Jayce, but the battle for the shore is no longer hopeless. Bridget inches toward safety, arms wrapped around the other woman, her muscles screaming.

"Holy shit!" a man shouts from the beach. "What the hell are you doing out there?"

"Help!" she cries, her voice raw and desperate as she keeps her partner's head above water. "Please! She's hurt!"

The strangers sprint forward to help as Bridget, trembling, drags Jayce from the water.

Epilogue

Jayce stands on the beach, wiggling her toes in the dry sand, smiling up at the sun. She closes her eyes, remembering their faces, the way they held each other, the way they loved each other. She remembers the warmth of their skin, the taste of their lips, the comfort of their words, and the pain—the blistering pain—that had rooted itself deep inside and made her body its home. She recalls the two women she'd never really met, but knew so completely.

She hopes, wherever they are, that they're at peace.

When she's done, she squeezes Bridget's hand, enjoying the way the silver wedding band presses against her skin.

"Are you ready?" Bridget asks with a smile.

"Ready."

"Three, two, one, toss!" she shouts.

The two women throw their small bouquets of violets, the naked flowers scattering apart in the wind. It's a ritual to mark how much they've overcome, and a way to remember a love that had been forgotten.

Bridget's flowers sail through the air before being swallowed up by a wave. Jayce's, on the other hand, don't go far. They land on the wet sand, the tide slowly pulling them out to sea.

Her body has yet to return to how it was before last spring and —if she's honest with herself—she knows it never will. Her shoulder is stiff, the mobility in her arm greatly reduced, and her scarred skin still hangs a bit too loose from her bones. She gets tired quickly, but struggles to stay asleep through the night, and there's a fragility to Jayce that never used to be there.

But she's also grown stronger in ways she never knew she could.

"Good to go?" Bridget asks, rubbing her arms to try and keep warm.

"Yeah, pretty much! I just need a second and then I'll be right behind you."

Bridget smiles and gives Jayce a peck on the cheek, making her way back up the beach.

Jayce looks out into the water. She can still feel a piece of Claudine deep inside of her. It's what makes her miss Marguerite on days like today, and why she finds herself drawn to violets.

Maybe one day, she'll return to the ocean.

She goes to step towards the water, her body called by it, but she catches herself and plants her foot back on the sand.

But not just yet.

"Ready?" Bridget asks.

Jayce nods and turns away from the crashing waves, smiling when she sees Bridget's hair billowing around her in the breeze, and heads towards her future.

About the Author

Caitlin Marceau is a queer Canadian author and illustrator known for her award-winning novella *This Is Where We Talk Things Out*. Her forthcoming work includes her debut novel, *It Wasn't Supposed To Go Like This*, and her second novella, *I'm Having Regrets*. For more, find her on social media at @CaitlinMarceau or check out CaitlinMarceau.ca.

Detailed Content Warnings

Body Horror
Vaginal Body Horror
Drowning
Immolation
Sexual Content
Homophobia (Implied)

www.ingramcontent.com/pod-product-compliance
Lightning Source LLC
Chambersburg PA
CBHW070426310726
48977CB00003B/854